Frederick H. Christian is the author of several *Sudden* westerns which have sold in hundreds of thousands all over the world. He has also written six other books in the bestselling *Angel* series.

An authority on the Old West, Mr. Christian's books are noted for their action, suspense and authenticity. He lives in Buckinghamshire.

Also by Frederick H. Christian and available from Sphere Books

KILL ANGEL
SEND ANGEL
FIND ANGEL
TRAP ANGEL
HANG ANGEL
FRAME ANGEL

Hunt Angel

FREDERICK H. CHRISTIAN

SPHERE BOOKS LIMITED
30/32 Gray's Inn Road, London WC1X 8JL

First published in Great Britain by Sphere Books Ltd 1975

TRADE MARK

Set in Intertype Plantin

Printed in Great Britain by
C. Nicholls & Company Ltd
The Philips Park Press, Manchester

For André

A NOTE TO THE READER

In Record Group 60 of the National Archives in Washington DC, there is abundant documentary evidence to the effect that for a number of years the Department of Justice employed a Special Investigator named Frank Angel, who was directly responsible to the Attorney-General of the United States. There is no record that any of the events in this book took place, or that Frank Angel took part in them. Equally, there is no record that he did not.

ONE

IN a way it was Cade's fault.

You couldn't blame him, of course, the poor sad bastard. It was getting so the Flying H boys couldn't come into town but Howie would stumble across their path, and sure as chickens lay eggs, they'd feel obliged to roust him up some. Not that it mattered; the Flying H boys had their fun but in the end they bought Howie the drinks he wanted, and so maybe each needed the other in some peculiar way. No harm done, usually, except that on this particularly hot, dusty Saturday night, Burt Hugess rode in with the boys, and he got to drinking like a man who meant to get drunk. Those citizens of Madison who'd seen Burt Hugess poison drunk – and that meant about everyone – quietly finished off their drinks and found good reasons to be elsewhere than the ornate precincts of Johnny Gardner's Palace Saloon. The Flying H boys soon had the place to themselves, which was just jim-dandy with them: as men a-horseback they had little enough time for the stiff-collared creeps who lived in town and ran the stores.

He was a big man, Burt Hugess: barrel-chested and powerful, shoulders like one of the fighting bulls you saw down in old Mexico. Bull-like, yes: everything about him. The way his head swung from side to side, the way his eyes had that red light behind them when he was mad, the thrusting, loping way he moved, all of them were bull-like, powerful. Yet it wasn't the sheer physical bulk of the man which alone made Johnny Gardner cringe as Burt Hugess' flat-hand pounded the mahogany bar for another drink. Lowering and ugly though Burt might be, there was a second reason to walk a big circle around him and that was the fact that he was the brother of Larry Hugess and Larry

Hugess owned this piece of Indian Territory as effectively as if he had branded every square foot of it personally with his Flying H iron.

The boys had been quiet enough to start with: Hugess and Danny Johnston and Johnny Evans and a couple of the Flying H wranglers, in off the dusty range for a Saturday night dust-cutting session. They were rowdy and they were rough but they spent freely and Johnny Gardner wasn't about to turn his patrician nose up at their cash money, not when so many of his customers seemed to think he could carry their slate indefinitely. Besides, he told himself, the boys never do any real harm, when you get right down to it. A few broken glasses, maybe. Once in a while a window shattered, someone scared shitless by an exuberantly-emptied sixgun. There was no malice in them, Gardner told himself, knowing as he did so that he was a bigger liar than Baron Munchausen.

When Howie Cade came in through the rear door, there was a jeering shout of welcome from Jimmy Finstatt, who was standing alongside Burt Hugess.

'Well, looky here!' he yelled. 'If it ain't deppity Cade!'

That gave them a big laugh. Howie Cade had once been Marshal Dan Sheridan's deputy, and a damned good one, too. Fast with a gun. A reliable man to have alongside you in a tight corner. But that had been in the days BL – Before Lily.

Lily had arrived in Madison the preceding fall on her way – she said – to open up a dressmaking business in Winslow. Well, if that was what she wanted to pretend, Madison really didn't mind. As to believing it, well, that was something else again, because Lily was quite obviously what she was, and if she'd been wearing a sign painted in red letters around her neck it couldn't have been any damned plainer and there wasn't a man in town who didn't know it. Correction: there was one man who didn't know it, didn't want to know it, and couldn't be told, and that man was

Howie Cade. He thought that Lily Elliott was just about the best thing that had happened to mankind since the invention of the wheel. He fell for Lily with a bang that could have been heard in four counties.

Now there were things a friend could do in situations like this, and Dan Sheridan, to his credit, did them all. He hinted a little, asked one or two of the right questions, pointed out – very gently, because he had no real desire to get into a fist-fight with Howie – the discrepancies in Lily's story; but to no avail. After that, he shrugged and gave up. Everyone had the right to go to hell in their own beautifully-fashioned handbasket, at least in Dan Sheridan's book. He had few enough friends as it was: telling Howie the naked truth was a sure way of losing another. Which meant, inevitably, that Howie found out the hard way.

Lily, as everyone expected, ran exactly true to form. She took Howie for every cent he'd saved in four years of keeping the law in Madison and then, like the Arabs, she folded her tents and departed. All of which would have been normal, understandable, unremarkable. They happened, such things. But Howie took it hard, very hard.

He started finding solace at the bottom of a glass, and then at the bottom of a bottle, and finally the bottle had him and he didn't give a damn. Sheridan figured it wasn't one of those how-could-she-do-a-thing-like-that-to-me cases, but a how-could-I-make-such-a-damned-fool-of-myself one. Howie was burying his shame, and at first Sheridan had figured he'd climb out of it, but Howie went deeper down, and in the end, Sheridan had to take the star off him because Howie was getting to be a liability. He gave his former deputy a job as a sort of caretaker in the jailhouse, sweeping the place out; paying Howie a few bucks a week for his efforts. He'd have cut his throat before he'd have admitted that he was paying the money out of his own pocket: he figured Howie's pride was battered enough. Not that it mattered: the money was never in Howie's jeans longer than the time it took him to drink it away, so for the rest of each week Howie hustled for a drink any way he could. Which was how he came inevitably into the orbit of the Flying H boys.

'Well, Howie,' Burt Hugess said, with silken contempt, 'you look like a man who needs a drink.'

A light kindled in Howie's eyes: part hope, part disbelief. Maybe Burt was in a good mood. Maybe the boys wouldn't roust him this time. It wasn't likely, but it was possible. He licked his lips, tasting the smoky burn of the whiskey already. The need was like dull aching fire in a void, a dying star imprisoned in his belly. *Oh, God,* he thought. *Let it be all right.* He slouched across to where Hugess was standing with his elbows on the bar, heel hooked in the brass rail.

'Jesus!' Hugess exclaimed, making a big production out of wrinkling his nose. 'Howie, you stink, you know that?'

The Flying H boys grouped around him laughed dutifully.

'Comes from sleepin' in the stable ever' night,' Johnny Evans grinned.

'Hell,' another said. 'I ain't never met no horse smelled *that* bad!'

''ceptin' a dead one,' Danny Johnston shouted, slapping his leg.

Burt Hugess sloshed more whiskey into his glass, letting Howie see him do it, taunting him with it. He drank greedily, feeling Howie's eyes on his bobbing Adam's apple, strength and a sense of power surging into him. The banked fires behind his eyes flared momentarily brighter, then died again. Some men drank and then sang. Others drank and slept or drank and laughed or drank and found themselves a *puta*; but not Burt Hugess. Burt was a mean drunk. Liquor fed a seething hot blackness inside him, raising its temperature slowly, inexorably, irresistibly. He looked at his huge hands, clenching them, flexing them. I could smash anything with them, he thought. It made him feel good.

'How about a drink, huh, Burt?' Howie whined. 'Just a small one, huh, Burt, just the one, lissen, I got a th—'

He had reached out a trembling hand towards Burt's bottle, his fingers almost touching it when the big man's hand clamped down on his skinny forearms like a vice, bringing a small shout of pain from Howie.

'Keep your smelly paws off my whiskey!' Burt snapped.

'Aw, Burt,' Howie wheedled. 'Lissen, just the one, lissen . . .'

'Get away,' Burt said, no anger in his voice. He knew just what he was doing. He turned his back on the cringing Howie and drew the bottle and glass towards him. Slowly, as if with loving care, he poured a generous drink. Then he picked up the glass, lifted it until the flaring light of the kerosene lamps was behind it, looking at the liquor with pursed lips like a wine-buyer judging a vintage. He let Howie look at it, too, and then, thirstily and with obvious enjoyment, Burt drank the whiskey down. He acted as though Howie wasn't there, as though he couldn't see his misery.

'Aw, Burt,' Howie begged. He put a hand on Hugess' forearm.

'Get your stinking paw off of me!' Burt said. There was that first faint thin thread of ugliness in the sound of his voice and Danny Johnston, recognising it, looked up quickly, his eyes narrowing. Everyone steered well clear of Burt when he was off on a mean drunk. Yet he still showed no sign of the fires raging below the surface and Johnston relaxed.

'Hey, Burt,' he said, light as a feather, 'take it easy, Burt.'

'Sure,' Burt grinned. 'Here, filth!'

He had a dollar in his hand, a silver dollar that caught the light from the lamps as Hugess flipped it up and then caught it. Then he flipped the coin again and this time he made no attempt to catch it and it thudded into the damp, bespittled sawdust on the floor. Howie Cade went on his knees, clawing for it, scrabbling to get it. The scream he gave when Burt Hugess stood on his hand made everyone jump. All the big man's weight was on his right foot for a very long moment while Howie looked up at him with eyes aching with agony and then Burt Hugess stepped back with pantomime contrition, making a gesture of apology.

'Aw, hell, Howie,' he said, 'did I stand on your fingers? I'm sorry, boy, it's just I never expected to find a man down there on the floor grovellin' in the dirt like some poxed-up halfbreed.'

Howie Cade looked at his scraped right hand and then at Hugess. He put the hand under his left arm, holding it gently for a moment, looking up at the big man with tears in his eyes. There was pain in them, too, and defeat, but way on back behind all of that there was something else, something Howie Cade hadn't felt for a long time – anger. The surge of the adrenalin was quite unexpected and he was moving before he realised it, coming up to his feet squalling like a cat with inarticulate rage. His sudden movement caught Burt Hugess momentarily off guard, but only for a moment. Then the huge paws moved, clamping Howie's purposelessly-clawing hands. Almost casually, Burt Hugess moved Howie's hands so that he could hold them one-handed, and then with the other hand, the right hand, he slapped Howie across the face, lightly, chastisingly at first and then harder and then harder until Howie's face was rocked right and then left and then right and then left and then Burt Hugess shoved him away against the surrounding ring of his men, and they shoved Howie back at Burt, jeering at him, and Burt slapped him back into their arms and they pushed him back again. Howie's face was cut to ribbons, his mouth a bloody tatter, eyes closing rapidly. All he could hear was the jeering and the flat meaty sound Burt Hugess' hand made when it hit him.

'Leave him be, Burt!'

Howie sank to the floor, stunned, hardly able to see but recognising the voice as that of Dan Sheridan's deputy, the man who had taken his place, Clell Black. He couldn't see Clell, only the legs of the Flying H riders and Burt Hugess' huge bulk in front of him.

'Get away from him, boys!' he heard Clell say. The deputy's voice was even, unhurried, not excited. Oh, Howie thought, and then he saw the gun in Burt Hugess' hand almost right in front of his eyes and the red flame blossomed from the barrel, the thunder of the shot deafening him. The Flying H men had moved, and Howie could see Clell Black, across the room near the door. The deputy hadn't even drawn his gun. He was looking down at the spreading stain on his chest with wide astonished eyes. Then all at once he seemed to deflate, to shrink. He slid almost noiselessly to the sawdusted floor.

'Jesus, Burt!' Danny Johnston breathed.

Hugess said nothing, although he grunted like a man who had just picked up a heavy load. Howie Cade stayed very very still, afraid even to move lest he remind Burt Hugess of his presence. The gun hung limp at Burt's side, gunsmoke curling from the barrel. There was a smell of cordite.

'Jesus, Burt,' Johnston said again. 'He never even went for his gun!'

'Sure he did,' Hugess said, and there was a snarl in his voice as he said it. He looked at Danny Johnston, at all of them, just holding their eyes with his burning gaze. 'Sure he did.'

'Well,' Johnston said.

'Give me a drink,' Hugess snapped. He turned to face the petrified Johnny Gardner, who had not taken his eyes off the bleeding body of deputy Black since it had stopped moving. He jumped when Hugess spoke, and slopped whiskey all over the mahogany before he got Burt's glass filled. There was a silence in the saloon that slices could have been cut off. Burt Hugess upended the whiskey glass and poured the fiery stuff down his throat as if it were so much water. Then he went out through the batwing doors and never even so much as looked at the sprawled body on the floor.

TWO

HE got off the train at Hays.

He was a tall man, built big and rangy, his wide shoulders straining the seams of the dusty grey suit. He had no luggage: just a bedroll and a good, if well-used saddle. He might have been a middling well-off rancher returning from the east, or a cattle buyer from one of the St. Louis packing plants, had it not been for a certain look around the eyes that said he was something other than these. Hays City wasn't a curious town, however; nobody paid any attention to the stranger, whose name was Frank Angel, or asked him what his line of work was. In fact, he was a Special Investigator for the United States Department of Justice but that wouldn't have meant anything to anyone in Hays. If you weren't something to do with cattle, wheat or the military, nobody in Hays had anything to talk to you about.

He'd come on the Kansas Pacific as far as Hays, which was as good a jumping-off place as any. In his heart of hearts, Angel knew that he was avoiding the possibility of opening old wounds, disinterring old memories that would be revived by seeing Abilene or Fort Larned, memories of the bloody events of long ago in which he had participated.*

He dickered with the man who ran the livery stable for perhaps an hour and came out of the discussion with a rangy roan, a solid horse with a deep chest and sturdy legs that carried its head high and wasn't rope-shy.

Two hours later he was well away from Hays, riding south as the sun climbed to its highest point in the brassy vault of the sky, not pushing the horse, letting it make a steady pace due south towards the faint smudge of purple on the far horizon that was the Wichitas. It was a long ride to Fort Griffin on the Brazos, but that was the last place

* Related in *Find Angel*

anyone had seen Mal Magruder and so that was where he was going to have to start.

Angel had been in Chicago when he got word from the Attorney-General's office of his assignment. The Department of Justice wanted Magruder. They wanted him very badly. There was the question of his ferrying repeating rifles out of New Orleans and across to the Llano Estacado to trade with the Comancheros. There was the question of his connexion with the Italian secret society, the Stoppaghera, who controlled the New Orleans waterfront. But most of all there was the question of a dead Justice Department investigator who'd been sent to bring Magruder in, and who'd been killed in a saloon brawl in Fort Griffin, Texas. By Magruder.

The fact that Magruder could be anywhere in the southwest, that he had not less than a million uncharted square miles to move around in, was not mentioned, any more than the fact that the Department had no photograph of the man they were looking for, no really worthwhile physical data at all. Angel knew better than to complain. If he'd been sitting in the big, high-ceilinged room in Washington where the Attorney-General had his office, he would have just nodded and got up and gone about trying to find Magruder. As if the Attorney-General were speaking, he heard the familiar, rasping voice.

'If we had that much information, we wouldn't need Special Investigators to get it, would we?'

Angel nodded to himself, smiling grimly. There was a saying at the rackety old building on Pennsylvania Avenue that housed the Justice Department: if it's sympathy you're looking for, you'll find it in the dictionary – just after shit and just before syphilis.

He came down the side of a long draw and let the horse pick its way to the crest on the far side. As the brown, baking plains below him, shimmering in the heat, came into full view, he saw the wagon train up ahead in the distance: five of them, moving across the empty land like strange insects. He gigged the horse forward. It would be pleasant to drink coffee in company instead of alone on the bare plains. Angel wasn't a gregarious man, but the soft sighing emptiness of the endless wind that keened across Kansas summer, winter, spring and fall depressed him, made him relive old dreams, fight forgotten wars again.

He came up on the wagons easy, letting them see him for a good long while as he drew closer. The lead wagon was being driven by a burly, red-faced man with a walrus moustache at least two sizes too big for him. He had a hefty wodge of chaw-tobacco working away in his right cheek, making him look like he had a gumboil. Every once in a while he'd spit at the mules, the gobbet *splacking* off the haunch of the unheeding animal in a glinting spray.

'That's a name musta given you trouble at school, sonny,' he roared.

'Did for a while,' Angel admitted. 'Till I got my growth.'

'Haw!' the wagonmaster shouted. 'Name's Ridlow. Nathan Stewart Lester Edward Ridlow. Nate when ya gits ta know me. Haw!'

He was from Fort Worth, he told Angel, and he made this trip four times a year, hauling supplies for the Fort Worth Mining Company from Hays, hauling copper ingots back up to the railroad.

'Be goddamned happier when they gits that new line a-builded,' he roared. 'Cut four days off of m' journey, haw!'

Angel suggested that it was a pretty monotonous trip to make four times a year: there wasn't enough scenery in the country between Fort Worth and Independence, Missouri to paint on a postage stamp.

'Wal,' Ridlow said, firing another great gobbet of tobacco-juice at the rump of the offside mule that went *splack!* and splattered just like all the others before it. 'Haw! Wal, it keeps a feller busy,' Ridlow said. 'Also don't see no more o' my old lady that I got to, haw!'

They camped that night on the open prairie.

Ridlow's drivers made a square out of the wagons and a rope corral was erected for the mules, which were also ground-hobbled. There wasn't too much likelihood of Indians, but the frontiersman's first rule was 'take no chances'.

After they had eaten, Angel asked the old wagonmaster about the sign they had passed as they crossed the dried-out ford at Bluff Creek. It had been a square of white boards, on which was painted in uncompromising capitals THIS IS FLYING H LAND. KEEP IT IN MIND.

'The Hugess ranch,' Ridlow told him. 'Biggest spread 'n these parts, bar none. Stretches clear on down to the Cimarron, on into Injun Territory. Take a man on a good horse two days to ride across 'er from east t'west, they say.'

In answer to Angel's next question, he frowned.

'Never met Larry Hugess, so can't say. Met his brother, though. Burt. Big sonofabitch. One o' them pizen drunks. Make a habit o' gettin' in deep trouble and then squawkin' for Larry, his brother, to come bail him out.'

'And does he?'

'Bail him out? Every damn' time, by cracky. Haw!'

'He must have a lot of clout in these parts.'

'Bet y'r ass,' Ridlow grinned toothlessly. 'He wrote the book. Haw!'

He started to rise, and then turned to the younger man.

'Welcome to ride with us tomorrow,' he said. 'All the damned way, come to that.'

THREE

BURT HUGESS walked down Front Street like a prowling lion.

He felt a strange elation, a Christmas Eve sort of anticipation, something coming. He felt ten feet tall and sexually aroused: he needed a drink and a girl and he could get both in Fat Mary's. He went down the street towards the depot with his head high and a proud, contained smile touching his mouth and people on the boarded sidewalks got out of his way, parting before him like water before the thrusting prow of a ship, as if they could feel some emanation, some aura about him. Word of the killing had preceded him down the street; nobody wanted to bump into Burt Hugess when he was killing drunk.

He went across the tracks and down the rutted track to Fat Mary's place. It was surrounded by an unlovely pile of trash, and half-clean clothing hung on a sagging line above the chickens foraging in the dirt. One long, low box of adobe: he went through the door into the cool darkness of a sort of hall, the earth damped down with sprinkled water. Facing the door was a bar of sorts: Fat Mary served only *tequila*. Off to each side were curtained apertures, through which you could walk down the corridor to one of the four cribs on each side. There were a couple of girls sitting around, idly fanning themselves, their Mother Hubbards hiked up high on their thighs. A young Spanish-looking fellow was playing a guitar softly but he stopped abruptly as Burt weaved in and pounded the bar. Fat Mary came bustling through the curtained doorway, and pasted a smile on her sweaty face when she saw who it was. A quick signal Burt didn't see sent the girls out of the place. The guitarist backed quietly into the yard outside.

'Hello, Burt, honey,' Fat Mary said, sliding a glass across the rough planking of her bar. Her immense body wobbled as she reached back on a shelf for the *tequila* bottle and poured him a drink.

Burt Hugess smiled at her to let her know it was all right, he wasn't going to make trouble.

'Have one yourself,' he said.

'Why, if you ain't a darlin' doll,' she gurgled. Her smile was as false as a drummer's expense account. When she poured the drinks she slopped *tequila* on the bar. If he noticed her uneasiness, Burt ignored it.

'Another,' he said.

She started to pour the drink and then she made a strange noise in her throat and he looked at her in puzzlement. She wasn't looking at him. She was looking past him and Burt cursed, whirling around, his hand flickering towards the holstered gun at his hip as Fat Mary dropped to the floor behind the bar with a solid thud.

When Burt Hugess saw who was standing in the doorway of the adobe he jerked his hand away from the gun as if it had suddenly grown red hot, lifting his arms, palms facing down to the floor, almost to shoulder level.

'Sheridan!' he growled.

Dan Sheridan was a tall man, maybe an inch over six feet. There wasn't an ounce of fat on him, but he weighed a good hundred and ninety. His dark blond hair was cut on the long side, although not the show-long of some of the blustering fools who wore the star. He wore tan woollen pants tucked into well-kept brown mule-ear boots, a dark blue cotton shirt, a soft leather belt and holster that looked as if it had been painted on him. His eyes, grey as a hunting wolf's, were cold and challenging and he held the double-barrelled Greener with the nine-inch barrels across his left forearm like a man who was itching to use it. The twin bores trained on his belly transfixed Burt Hugess.

'Sheridan!' he said again.

He tried to will himself to act, to challenge the lawman, but every nerve and sinew denied the commands of his brain. He could see nothing except the imaginary picture of his body torn to ribbons by the buckshot that would riddle him if Sheridan pulled the triggers of the shotgun.

'All right,' Sheridan said at last. 'Unbuckle your gunbelt and stand away from it. You know the drill.'

Hugess didn't move. Sheridan took three steps forward and jammed the barrels of the gun into the big man's gut, pushing a noisy grunt from his slightly-open mouth. Close to, Burt Hugess could see the just-controlled rage seething beneath the apparently calm exterior and he realised Sheridan was inch-close to killing him like a mad dog. He swallowed noisily, eyes shuttling away from Sheridan's glare.

'I'll count three,' Sheridan said.

'Don't bother,' said a voice behind him.

Sheridan's eyes widened a fraction. Hugess could see him think about it.

'I could still take Burt with me,' Sheridan said, almost conversationally, to the men behind him.

'You do that and Larry Hugess will ride in here and burn this town down for your marker,' Danny Johnston said, reminding Sheridan of his own position with a jab of the cocked sixgun. Burt Hugess saw the lawman's shoulders droop fractionally, and he knew the danger was over. He snatched the shotgun out of Sheridan's hands, breaking it open and kicking the bright red shells out of sight.

'Lean on the bar, both hands!' he snapped.

Sheridan just looked at him, the way a man might look at a reptile.

'Do it,' Danny Johnston said behind him.

Sheridan shrugged. He leaned forward, both arms stretched out, hands on the front angle of the bar keeping him upright. The other Flying H riders pushed into the adobe. They wanted to see the fun.

Sheridan looked at them. Danny Johnston, Johnny Evans,

Ken Finstatt, two others. He knew them all, made a mental note. While he was doing it, Burt Hugess moved like a cat and whacked the barrels of the shotgun down like an axe across the knuckles of Sheridan's right hand. Sheridan shouted with the pain and went down on his knees, writhing on the dirt floor, agony contorting his features. Burt Hugess dragged his own sixgun out and cocked it, pointing it at Sheridan's head.

'No, Burt!'

The shout made Hugess stop, whirling around to face the doorway where the tatterdemalion figure of Howie Cade stood with a sixgun in his hand. The Flying H riders had turned, too, and now Danny Johnston's voice cut the silence, contemptuous.

'Get out of here, you bum,' he snapped, turning away.

Burt Hugess was already turning back to Sheridan, who was on the floor looking up at him now.

'All right,' Burt said.

The sound of the shot was shockingly loud in the small area but it did not come from Burt's sixgun. Howie Cade let fly from the doorway and his carefully-placed bullet took Burt Hugess high on the meaty part of his right shoulder, slamming the big man's brawny form against the bar, and capsizing it on top of the screeching woman hiding behind it. Burt slid off the fallen bar with the bright blood breaking across his upper body, eyes astonished. The Flying H riders looked from the fallen man to Howie Cade, standing in the doorway with a smoking Smith & Wesson steady as a rock in his hand, and Danny Johnston said 'What in the name of hell . . .?'

He realised that he still had the sixgun in his hand and as he did so Howie Cade spoke.

'I want that gun on the floor, Danny,' Howie said. 'And I do mean now!'

'Shit, Howie,' Danny Johnston said. 'You can't take all of us.' The gun in his hand didn't move, but Johnny Evans and the others, without moving, became poised for movement.

'I can shoot your balls off,' Howie reminded Johnston. His voice cracked on the last word.

'Misdoubt you could make it, boy,' Johnny Evans said, silky-soft.

It looked like he might be right. Whatever impulse had driven Howie Cade to action, it was gone. The resolution was dribbling out of him visibly like sand from a broken egg-timer. He suddenly looked old, grey, and very tired; the hand holding the sixgun trembled visibly.

'You wanna kill him or shall I?' Danny Johnston said to Johnny Evans.

Howie watched them, the gun moving in a small arc between the two men, his eyes full of desperate apprehension.

'Don't make me kill you, Danny!' he said. His voice was smaller, too. The Flying H men could hear the difference.

'Shit, Johnny, you kill him,' Johnston said, as if disgusted.

They had forgotten Sheridan. He'd been out of it, on the floor, his hand all shot to hell, done with as far as they were concerned. It was a bad mistake because Sheridan had reached across his own body and had the Colt .44-40 with the four-and-a-half-inch barrel in his left hand. The sound it made when he cocked it was like a thunderclap and the five Flying H men froze.

'As I was saying,' Howie Cade said, all the life coming back into his eyes. 'I want that gun on the floor, Danny.'

Johnston thought it over for a fast count of three and then dropped the gun. It made a soft thud in the dirt.

'Now the rest of you boys,' Howie said softly. 'Shuck your belts and step away from them.'

Johnny Evans looked at Sheridan. The marshal was on his feet now and he looked as if he'd welcome an excuse to use the gun in his hand.

'Do what he says,' Sheridan rasped.

Howie Cade watched the Flying H men unbuckle their belts and step shamefacedly away from them. Nobody spoke. Outside in the street they could hear the sound of wagons rumbling across the wooden boards that bridged the railroad track.

'Now get the hell out of town,' Sheridan said.

Danny Johnston shrugged, and then stepped forward as though to help Burt Hugess to his feet. Sheridan stopped him with a gesture of the Colt.

'What . . .?' said Danny, puzzled.

'He's under arrest,' Sheridan said. 'For murder.'

'Are you serious?'

'You want to try me?'

'You know what'll happen, Sheridan? You know what Larry Hugess will do to you? He'll cut you up for jerky!'

'That'll be the day,' Sheridan said. 'On your way, boys.'

'Listen, Sheridan, Burt needs a doctor. He's hurt,' Evans put in.

'Can't you see how I'm worrying about him?' Sheridan grinned, cold as charity.

He gestured with the sixgun, and this time the Flying H boys moved, filing past Howie Cade without meeting his eyes. They got on their horses and yanked them into movement, cutting across the northern side of the railroad depot and leaving only a softly sifting cloud of dust in their wake. Howie Cade had followed them outside and watched them go. Now he came back into Fat Mary's.

'Jesus,' he said. He was trembling. 'I need a drink.'

Sheridan was hauling Burt Hugess to his feet. Burt looked ashen, shocked. His arm hung at his side like a piece of string. His shirt was stiff with dried blood. He watched with dull eyes as Howie went across to the shelves behind the bar which Fat Mary had propped up again and lifted down a bottle of *tequila*. Fat Mary watched him with eyes like a snake but she said no word. Neither did Sheridan.

Howie uncorked the bottle and poured himself a stiff

drink. He looked at it for a long moment, lifted it, smelled it. Then he poured it on the floor. He looked at Sheridan and tried for a grin which didn't stick on too well.

'We better go get Doc Franklin to take a look at that hand of yours,' he said.

'Yeah,' Sheridan said. He looked at his hand. It was swollen into a ball, bruised blue here and there, with darkened patches of dried blood beneath the skin. He couldn't move any of the fingers at all. Great shape to take on the full strength of the Flying H, he thought grimly. He looked at Howie Cade.

'Thanks,' he said.

'Aw,' Howie said. 'Listen, let's get the hell outa here.'

He knew what Sheridan was thinking. He was thinking it himself. A town marshal without a gun hand plus a deputy who might get through the night without taking a drink was a poor combination to put up against what Larry Hugess would start rolling when Danny Johnston and his boys got back to the Flying H. He gave Burt Hugess a prod with his sixgun.

'Okay, tiger,' he grinned. 'Let's go.'

The three of them went out of there and across the tracks, walking Burt Hugess up the street towards the jail. They walked in the centre of the street, letting the whole town see them. Sheridan hoped he didn't look as worried as he felt. Howie's nickname for Hugess wasn't misplaced. He had a tiger by the tail, all right. And only one good hand to hold on with.

FOUR

MADISON was no great shakes as a town.

There were a thousand like it, and Frank Angel sometimes had the feeling he'd seen most of them. Madison's two streets, Front and Texas, joined each other in a T-junction, Front being the horizontal. At the northern end of Front was the railroad depot and the flat-roofed, gloomy-windowed warehouse owned by the Hugess outfit. Along its slab adobe sides in six-foot white capitals was painted the legend 'L & B Hugess, Traders & Merchants'. Upon a bluff above the depot and set back maybe a hundred yards from the main street was a small white frame church with a neat graveyard behind it. Almost directly opposite the pathway leading to the church was another pathway that wound down behind the breaks and across the tracks to the huddle of shacks and adobes that housed such establishments as Fat Mary's. Front Street boasted the usual livery stable, a two-storey building that housed a restaurant and also let rooms, and almost opposite Texas Street, Johnny Gardner's Palace Saloon. At the southern end of Front, there was a wooden bridge across Cat Creek, down to a mere trickle at this time of year. The bridge was a duplicate of the one which crossed the same creek at the eastern end of Texas Street, in which – if you cared, which frankly Angel didn't – you could find the general store and another saloon, the Oriental, and, opposite it on the junction of Front and Texas, the marshal's office and the jailhouse in their solidly-constructed adobe with its heavy iron studded oak door and barred windows.

There weren't many people about.

Angel rode the roan south on Front towards the bridge across the creek, his mind on his destination and his task there; he'd left Ridlow, after an evening of quiet drinks together, with his wagons in the big corral in back of the general store where Ridlow had taken them last night. The town had been abuzz with the news of the marshal's arrest of Burt Hugess, everyone pretty well agreeing that Sheridan was about to find out what it was like to walk bare-assed through Hell. The threat of the Hugess outfit hung over the place like a black cloud but Angel had closed his mind to it: the Department had a rule, and the rule was *don't get involved.* If it didn't directly bear upon the job you had in hand, you rode around it, you ducked it, you walked away from it, you got out of it any damned way you could, but you didn't get involved. The Justice Department had its own fish to fry and they didn't include the problems of a town marshal in some Godforsaken wide spot in the road, no matter how pressing.

There were some men standing idly at the town end of the bridge. They had the peculiarly unoccupied look of waiters in a failing restaurant. Angel's sharp glance noted that all of them were carrying carbines, and all wore heavy belts of ammunition looped over their shoulders. As he approached the bridge one of the men slouched out into the middle of the road and stood there watching him come nearer. At about ten yards the man spoke. 'All right, cowboy,' he said. 'Turn around.'

He was about thirty, thickset, face stubbled with a three-day beard. He wore a red shirt and tight-fitting Levi pants. He had his shirt sleeves rolled back halfway between elbow and wrist, kind of fanciful; and he wore two sixguns in holsters peculiarly canted forward so that the gun butts hung back not far from the horizontal.

'What is this?' Angel asked mildly.

'Just turn around,' the man said. 'Nobody leaves town.'

Angel just looked at him for a long moment and in that long moment one of the other men eased away from the wooden stanchion against which he had been leaning. He laid the barrel of his Winchester idly across his forearm so that the muzzle pointed directly at the man on horseback.

'Mind telling me why?' Angel asked. 'I got to be in Fort Griffin—'

'Forget it!' said Red Shirt. He let a leer touch his lips. 'She'll wait or she won't. Right, Harvey?'

'Right,' said the man with the Winchester. He was still watching Angel with the wary eyes of a man who's been caught off his guard once and never will be again if he can help it.

'You boys work for Larry Hugess?' Angel said.

'Yeah, what of it?'

'Why does he want the town locked up?'

'You a stranger here, sonny?' sneered Red Shirt.

'Came in last night,' Angel said.

'You hear about the fracas – about Burt Hugess gettin' arrested?'

'Uh-huh.'

'So.'

'So how does that affect me?'

'Jesus,' Red Shirt exploded. 'Why do we always got to explain to them?'

'Tell him,' said the other one.

'All right,' grouched Red Shirt. 'It's like this, see, cowboy.' He made his speech patient, simple, the way he might talk to a small child or someone touched in the head. 'Marshal Sheridan arrested Burt Hugess, and Larry Hugess don't like that. He aims to show Mister Sheridan what it's like to be caught atween a rock and a hard place. But he aims to do it without no interference. That means no messengers heading over for Winslow to get the U.S. Marshal, or to Fort Supply for the so'jer boys. Sheridan's got hisself into this, and Larry Hugess aims to let him try gettin' hisself out of it. All on his ownsome. Now you savvy?'

'Suppose, Angel said. 'Just suppose, mind you – that I was inclined to argue the point.'

'That'd be an error,' the man with the Winchester said quietly.

'Look!' said Red Shirt.

He moved. Angel knew that he'd moved and yet couldn't truly say he'd seen the movement yet the man had the right-hand sixgun in his hand, cocked. It was faster than anything Angel had ever seen and he had seen some of the very best men in the business.

'Got you,' Angel nodded. He pulled around the horse's head, and over his shoulder, he said: 'You boys got any idea how long I got to be holed up in this burg?'

'Don't make any long-term bookin',' Winchester said, with a coarse cackle.

He'd already ported the carbine, and Red Shirt had re-holstered the sixgun in the strangely-canted holster at his side. Angel walked the horse back up Front Street, heading for the hotel. As he got level with Texas Street he saw Ridlow standing on the sidewalk gesticulating violently at a tall, contained-looking man whose right arm was in a bandanna sling, and whose sixgun was stuck in his waistband on the right hand side for a cross-draw. The Marshal, Angel told himself. He swung down from the roan outside the jail.

'Here, Frank!' Ridlow turned towards him. 'You know what happened?'

'Some jaspers stopped you leaving town,' Angel said.

'Aw,' Ridlow said, disappointed at not being able to voice his disgust again for Angel's benefit. 'Yo're damned tootin' they did. An' I wanna know what in thunder's going on. Oh, Dan Sheridan, Marshal o' this place, Frank. This's Frank Angel, Dan.'

Sheridan nodded an acknowledgement of the introduction. He had dark shadows beneath his eyes. Pain? A sleepless night? Both, perhaps, Angel thought.

'Them Hugess boys got this town locked up tighter'n a rattler's ass, Dan,' Ridlow continued. 'What you aimin' to do about 'er?' He awaited Sheridan's reply with a belligerent expression on his face. It turned to sour disgust as Sheridan answered with a shrug.

'Shee-hit, boy, you can't just let Hugess take over yore town!' Ridlow snapped.

'Got any suggestions, Nathan?' the Marshal asked, mildly. His thoughts seemed to be elsewhere, as though he was merely being pleasantly polite to Ridlow.

'Wall,' Ridlow said. He let loose a burst of tobacco juice that soared half-way cross the street and *splatted* in the shifting dust. 'Reckon mebbe me an' my boys better pitch in an' help you out, some. Haw!'

For the first time decision came into Sheridan's eyes. He shook his head, frowning down on the old man.

'Thanks, Nathan, but no. No way. You and your boys keep out of this!'

'Hell, Sheridan,' Ridlow snapped. 'You need all the help you can git!'

'No offence,' Sheridan said. 'Nathan, how good are you with a gun?'

'Wall,' Ridlow said. 'Haw!' He let go with another splatter of cud. 'If'n you're askin' me whether I'm a gunfighter or not, boy, well – haw! I ain't!'

'I can't recall I ever saw you carrying a pistol, Nathan.'

'Wall, shoot, boy, I know what end to point! Haw!'

'You good enough to go up against Willie, Nathan? Willie Johns?'

'Aw, hell,' Ridlow said. 'You know damned well ain't nobody goin' to go up agin' that snake-hipped sonofabitch, Sheridan!'

'Willie Johns,' Angel said. 'Is he a thickset fellow, medium height, heavy stubble, wears his guns kind of tilted, so?'

'That's him,' Sheridan said, looking at Angel and seeing him for the first time. 'Why?'

'Nothing,' Angel said. 'I think I just met him. He gave me a demonstration of how fast he can pull a sixgun.'

'Tell your friend here,' Sheridan said heavily. 'Maybe

he'll believe you. Me, I already know how fast friend Johns is.'

He turned back to face Nathan Ridlow.

'So you just keep your nose clean, Nathan,' he said. 'You pitch into this, you'd be just one more for me to look out for. And I've got all the problems I can use.'

'Hell, I guess yo're right, Dan,' Nathan Ridlow said. 'Just goes an' sticks in my craw that th'only backup you got is that boozehead.'

As he spoke, Howie Cade came to the door of the jail. There was no way he could not have heard what Ridlow said, but the old man didn't back up one inch. He glared at Howie as though he was daring him to take offence at what was the plain truth for any eye to see. Indeed, Howie Cade looked like something that had been chawed on and spat out. His clothes were ragged, filthy. He needed a shave and a haircut and a bath, not necessarily in that order. His hands were shaky and his eyes looked like he'd just ridden through a dust storm.

'I need a drink,' he told Sheridan.

'Sure,' Sheridan said, gently. 'Go on down the street. Maybe one of the Hugess boys will buy you one.'

'A beer would do,' Howie said.

'Got some inside,' Sheridan grinned, putting his deputy out of his agony. 'While you were asleep. Figured you'd need something when you came up for air.'

He turned and opened the door clumsily with his left hand.

'You boys like to join us?' he said to Ridlow and Angel.

'Try an' stop us!' Ridlow cackled. 'Haw!'

The jail was simply built. The square building was divided down its middle by a corridor. On the street side of the corridor was the marshal's office, fenced off from the rest of the room by a low rail with a swinging door in it. There was a pot-bellied stove in one corner of the room, two rifle racks with shotguns and carbines chained in them and locked, a cupboard, and a scarred old desk with a swivel chair behind it that had seen better days. In the open area was another, equally decrepit desk and chair for the deputy. Between his desk and Sheridan's a door opened into the corridor, on the corral side of which were three cells. Burt Hugess was in the middle one: the other two were empty.

Sheridan went around behind his desk and reached down into the cool corner of the adobe walls; he came up with a heavy earthenware jug that had a damp cloth stretched across its mouth. He pointed with his chin at some tin cups hanging on nails along the side of the cupboard, and Nathan Ridlow planked them down one, two, three, four on Sheridan's desk, licking his moustache as the cool beer foamed into them. While he and Angel were saluting the Marshal, Howie Cade emptied his cup like a man who's lived through a drought. He looked up, sheepishly, when he felt their eyes on him.

'I'm all right,' he said, defensively. 'Just thirsty.'

But his eyes pleaded with Sheridan, who nodded and filled his deputy's cup again. They tried not to watch Howic struggling to drink it slowly.

'Where have you got Hugess?' Angel asked, more to fill the silence than anything else.

'Back there, in the middle cell,' Sheridan said, jerking his head towards the half-open door to the corridor. 'Nice and comfortable.' He raised his voice a couple of lungfuls. 'Aren't you, Burt?'

'Go to hell, Sheridan!' shouted the prisoner.

'Nice fellow,' Sheridan smiled. 'Like his brother.'

'No sign of him turning up yet?'

'Nope.'

'He'll be here!' Burt Hugess shouted from the cell. 'Bet on that!'

'You want to know the truth, I wish he'd get at it,' Howie Cade muttered. 'We nailed Burt twelve hours ago and so far nothing's happened.'

'Well, hardly,' Sheridan said, and told him about the barricades at the exits from town. Angel watched the deputy's face grow tight and pale as the Marshal spoke.

'We could lock 'em all up,' Howie said, not really believing it. Sheridan just looked at him with one of those you-know-better-than-that looks.

'Even if you could – an' you can't – Hugess'd just send another passel o' gunnies in,' Nathan Ridlow said. 'Haw!'

Angel said nothing, but he recognised the Marshal's dilemma: damned if he did nothing, damned equally if he made a move. If Sheridan held on to Burt Hugess, then Larry Hugess would take him out of jail by force. If he turned Burt loose, they'd ride him out of town on a rail and he'd never get a job policing a town anywhere again as long as he lived, even if he did get so he could one day look himself in the eye again. Some parlay: a one-handed lawman and a dipso deputy up against the combined weight of Hugess and his riders. In the back of his mind he heard the warning voice of the Attorney-General, imagined himself again in the big, high-ceilinged room overlooking Pennsylvania Avenue in Washington with its disordered bookshelves and its drooping flags.

'You know the rule, Angel,' the Old Man would say. 'Keep out of it.'

'But I need to move out,' he would argue. 'After Magruder. Every day I lose gives him a longer head-start.'

'Can't be helped,' the Attorney-General would reply. 'Not as if it's forever.'

'But—'

'This . . . problem,' the Attorney-General would go on, giving him no chance to argue. 'Happens all the time, right? Frontier towns are pretty much all the same, are they not? Always someone struggling to be top dog, am I correct?'

And Angel would nod, because it was true, even if in this case . . .

'I know what you're going to say now,' the Attorney-

General would say, reaching for one of the long cigars he smoked. 'This is different.'

'It is,' Angel would say. 'You see—'

'No difference at all,' would come the interruption, sharp through the billowing folds of stinging smoke from the cigar. Department wags said that there was a $5000 bounty for the man who could find the Attorney-General's cigar-maker – and kill him before he made any more. 'Tell me how this one is different. Town marshal handling a local problem. No Federal laws broken: always supposing we could make Federal law stick in Indian Territory. Could be argued, I suppose, that a town Marshal hasn't any true legal right to arrest anyway. Citizen's arrest, nothing more. And nothing to do with this Department, Frank.' Each word emphasised by a jab from the cigar.

'Agreed?'

And Angel would duck his head, agreeing.

'Then don't get involved.'

He pulled his thoughts back to the here and now, heard Sheridan saying that the only thing he could usefully do was to sit tight and wait to see what Hugess planned.

'Wall,' Ridlow said. 'Damned if I'm gonna sit around waitin' on him. I'm gonna round up some able bodies an'—'

'Nathan!' Sheridan said. His voice was not loud, but it stopped Ridlow's chatter like a tap being turned. 'Just – plain – don't. And that's an order!'

Old Ridlow looked at the Marshal, and then at Howie Cade, and then back at the Marshal.

'Aw,' he said. 'Hell, Dan'l, if that's the way you feel.'

'That's the way I feel,' Sheridan said. 'And don't you forget it.'

'Shoot,' Ridlow said. 'Then that's the way she'll be. How about one more afore I get on about my business? Just a leetle one. Haw!'

Sheridan poured the beer into the cups. He handled the

job quite well but it was plain to Angel that the Marshal wasn't used to using his left hand and that he'd be somewhere less than fast getting his gun into action if he had to. As for using a rifle . . . it was better not to think too much about it. Don't get involved, he told himself again.

When they'd finished the beer, he got up to leave with Ridlow, telling himself that what he'd do was wait it out, see what happened. He could always pitch in alongside Sheridan if they hit the jail. He decided to hold on until nightfall before making a decision but the way it turned out he didn't have to make any decision at all. It was made for him at around seven-thirty that night when someone cut Nathan Ridlow down from ambush in an alley halfway up Front Street.

FIVE

RIDLOW hadn't even been wearing a gun.

He'd spent most of the later afternoon and early evening going from store to saloon to restaurant to livery stable to saloon, haranguing the citizens of Madison to support their Marshal, completely ignoring the warning that Sheridan had served on him. He'd been vituperative, scalding, merciless, calling Madison's menfolk spineless, spavined, swaybacked, and possessed of less guts than a cooked rainbow trout, but all to no avail. When he had suggested a frontal attack on the Flying H riders, he had been gently reminded of the presence of such trigger-happy gunslingers as Danny Johnston and Willie Johns. When he had put up the idea of sending out riders in every direction under cover of darkness, it had taken only moments for someone to remind him that even if they escaped the town, the riders would still have to traverse Flying H range throughout the night, range patrolled by heavily-armed Hugess riders no doubt looking for just such riders, not to say hoping to encounter them. When, in disgust, he finally stamped out of the Oriental with the flat-stated intention of going the hell on down to the railroad depot and send him off a telegraph message to Fort Worth so at least his boss would know what the Sam Hill was holding him up, the citizens of Madison who'd had to stand still for his tongue-lashing watched him go with a mixture of shame and relief.

Nathan Ridlow stamped down the street towards the railroad depot, his temper not really gone at all: he'd whipped himself up into a good anger to tongue-lash the men in the bar, but in actual fact he wasn't truly angry, hadn't really expected them to rally round Sheridan. After all, they were shopkeepers, small business men, not gunslingers. The whole idea of hiring Sheridan was so he could do their gunslinging for them. If he got himself a tiger by the tail, it was his job to unhitch himself with the least possible damage to (a) the town and (b) its citizens, and not necessarily in that order.

'Which same is some trick,' he told himself, as he stomped down the boarded sidewalk. 'Haw!' He stopped as he stepped down from the boards on to the dusty ground just before the point where the side path going up to the church split off from the main street and in doing so, threw the aim of the ambushers. The lance of flame speared from the alley alongside the livery stable and Nathan Ridlow felt as if some huge, invisible being had punched him heavily on the upper chest. He was astonished to find himself face down in the dust of Front Street, and he could hear the deep repeated *whang!* of a Winchester carbine. Out of pure instinct he rolled over, trying for the shadow of the boardwalk off which he had just stepped. Now the sharper bark of a sixgun laid itself over the repeated roar of the carbine and bullets smacked gouts of dust into the old man's eyes and face, half-blinding him. Then the roar of the carbine turned into a terrible clanging sound, as if someone had smote a huge anvil right next to his head, very close. He could hear the metal vibrating and there was the taste of iron in his mouth. He cried out from the shock of it, not knowing that his body had been slammed back against the wall of the house behind him, not knowing yet that he was gutshot and dying.

'Goddammit all to hellangone!' he shouted and got up and ran.

He ran towards the church, grabbing at his belly instinctively, knowing somehow that he was all shot to hell down there, seeing the white frame building with its red-tiled roof through a blur of misting crimson that floated up over his eyes as if he was sinking in it. He went down on his knees and he heard someone shouting behind him.

'Kill the old fucker!' the voice yelled and he knew who it

was and then something went off like a firecracker in his head and he thought that's all, I'll never—

Dan Sheridan was already out in the street and running towards the sound of the shots. People were poking their heads out of windows, doorways, eyes seeking movement and the source of the shooting. The twilight was coming up from the creek-bed like a thief, gradually stealing the nearest ground. The alleys between the buildings were already in black shadow and Sheridan ran harder, suddenly aware of his own vulnerability, Cade back in the jail and nobody to back him if the Flying-boys stepped out on to the street and made him fight.

As he reached the path that led up the slight rise to the church, he checked, eyes swinging left and right. Nothing. No movement that he could see. A trap?

'Marshal!' someone called. 'Up here!'

The voice came from up the bluff, towards the church.

'Who is that?' He cocked the gun in his left hand.

'Phil Petrie, Marshal,' the man shouted. 'It's Nate. I think he's dead.'

Sheridan ran up the slope towards Petrie, who was kneeling over the body of Ridlow, which lay aflounder on the hard-packed earth. The side of the old man's head was a mangled mess of broken bone and tissue.

'You see what happened?' Sheridan snapped. Petrie was one of Ridlow's men.

Petrie shook his head. 'I was coming up the street, heard the shootin',' he said. 'I saw the boss roll down, as if he was hit. Then he got up and run up the hill. Someone shouted to get him and then he went down like a log.'

'Where did the shooting come from?'

'Over by the livery, 's far as I could tell,' Petrie said, jerking his head at the bulking loom of the stable across the other side of Front Street.

Sheridan looked up quickly as he heard someone coming

up the pathway fast: he had the gun ready, still cocked. He let down the hammer when he saw who it was.

'Is he dead?' Angel asked.

For answer, Sheridan scraped a match on his bootheel. By the flickering flame Angel could see the black blood that stained the entire middle of the old man's back, and the awful gaping mess that had been the side of his head.

'In the back,' Sheridan said, straightening up. 'But why?'

'He was shooting his mouth off in the saloon, Marshal,' Petrie said. 'Tellin' everyone what gutless wonders they was. Said he aimed to get word to Fort Worth as to why we was hung up here.'

'Ah,' said Sheridan, as though that explained it all.

He turned and looked down the slope towards the livery stable. Dark and squat, it was silent, menacing. He measured it all out with his eyes, the old man down there in the street, the men at the side of the stable, the shots, the staggering run towards the church . . . Old Ridlow had been given about as much chance as a steer in an abattoir.

'Anybody come out of there, Petrie?' Sheridan said. Petrie looked up, startled by the wicked rasp in Sheridan's voice.

'Out the stable?'

'Out of the stable.'

'No, sir, nobody,' Petrie said.

'You think they might still be in there?' Angel asked.

Sheridan looked at him as though Angel had just sprung from the ground, a touch of annoyance in his eyes. He put the barrel of the sixgun against Angel's upper arm and then put pressure on it, moving Angel to one side as if he were some weird new form of obstruction.

'I want to help,' Angel said, quietly.

'Sure,' Sheridan replied. 'Then get your friend Ridlow out of here.'

'No,' Angel said.

Sheridan looked at him again, differently this time. His eyes were empty, and Angel knew how he felt: it was the look of the man who knows he is going to get killed but can do no other thing.

'You join in now, you can't stop there,' Sheridan said. 'They'll mark you down.'

'I know that,' Angel said. 'That's why they killed the old man, wasn't it?'

'Right,' Sheridan said. 'A warning. In case anyone in town was thinking of helping me.'

He looked down at the body of Nathan Ridlow and then he started down the slope, not looking to see if Angel was following. Sheridan had one sixgun in his hand and another stuck in his waistband and he crossed the street in shadow and eased along the side of a house next to the livery stable until the stable was there in front of him, maybe fifteen feet away. There was a window high on the alley side of the stable; no doors. They were in front and back, the rear ones opening into a fenced corral in which half a dozen horses stood.

'Front or back?' Angel said. Sheridan turned to look at him, not letting the surprise show too much, but glad someone was with him.

'How do you feel?'

'They're hoping you'll do this, you know,' Angel said.

'I know.'

'Then take the front. Go in fast and hit the floor as soon as you do. They may not be expecting anyone to come in from the back.'

'All right,' Sheridan said. 'What for a signal?'

Angel did an owlhoot. It was pretty good, and Sheridan managed a tight smile.

'Okay,' he said, and went across the open space to the wall of the stable fast and low. Nothing happened. He eased around the front corner of the building, seeing Angel move quartering towards the corral like a shadow and the thought crossed his mind that maybe Angel wasn't just a passing drifter but then it was gone as he put all his thoughts aside and emptied everything out of himself except the cold readiness to move when he heard Angel's signal.

Whoo-hoo.

Sheridan ran across the face of the livery stable and out into Front Street, turning in a tight arc to smash the full weight of his right shoulder and body against the double doors, wincing as the impact jarred his broken hand, diving flat on the pocked-dusty floor of the stable, eyes wide to get the darkness out of them, sixgun up and cocked in his left hand.

Nothing.

He eased forward slightly and as he did, a shot from somewhere high up whanged out, smacking dust up into his face, forcing him to roll fast to one side as a second, a third, a fourth shot smashed downwards, the slugs seeking his body as he banged against one of the wooden stall partitions, bringing down a set of harness with a jingling thud.

He was getting carefully to his feet when Angel came in through the rear doors, moving very fast and already having set up his aim for the man up in the rafters of the stable, using the flashes of the man's gun to fix the spot. Angel moved across the door aperture from left to right, his body going backwards on to his shoulders, the sixgun in his right hand spitting fire as he fanned the hammer in a continuous roar, offering the man above no target, no chance. The five slugs were fired in a tight four-inch arc and the man in the rafters went up like a diver on a high board as the first caught him in the belly, the second just above the breastbone and the third underneath his jaw at the point where it hinges below the ear. He came down with a solid thud that sent flickering specks of chaff spiralling in the still warm air, but Frank Angel wasn't even looking at the man. He knew he was dead. He was jamming fresh shells into his sixgun and running towards Sheridan, and Sheridan paused, puzzled, then Angel shouted 'Behind you!' and he whirled to see the dark running form going out through the doorway and without thinking, without aiming, Sheridan let the hammer of the Colt go and he saw the man flinch, knew he'd hit him.

The two of them stood there in the acrid, cordite-stinking darkness.

'All right,' Angel said. He said it as though it was a decision, the end of something or the beginning. He went over to the man lying in the middle of the stable and turned him over with the toe of his boot. Sheridan came across as he struck a match and looked down at the mess of the man's face.

'Dick Ryan,' Sheridan said.

'Hugess rider?'

'What else?' Sheridan said. 'I think I clipped the second one.'

'Uh huh,' Angel said. 'Where would he hunt cover?'

Sheridan shrugged.

'I'd say the Palace. They got rooms over: for the riders, that is.'

'Would they take him there?'

'It's not likely.'

'Let's try the Palace,' Angel said. 'You can check out the jail on the way.'

Sheridan looked at him as they came out into the street.

'Listen,' he began.

'Don't bother,' Angel said. 'I promised myself I wasn't going to get involved. Wouldn't have done, either. Except for the old man. I liked him.'

'Either way, I'm thanking you,' Sheridan said.

'Thank me when it's over,' Angel said. 'Which sure as hell isn't yet.'

He started down Front Street and Sheridan lengthened his stride to match Angel's pace. There were people on the front porch of the Oriental. They looked at the two men as though they were dinosaurs.

'Look at them,' Sheridan said. 'Sheep!'

'Don't be too rough on them,' Angel said. 'It's not what they're good at.'

'You,' Sheridan said. 'Where'd you learn—?'

He stopped, aware that he wasn't observing good manners.

'It's all right,' Angel grinned. 'I'm not on the dodge.'

They were outside the jail now. Howie Cade was at the doorway, and he had Sheridan's sawn-off Greener comfortably cradled across his arm.

'Havin' fun?' he said sardonically, as they got nearer. 'Enjoyin' yourselves?'

'Ginger peachy,' Angel grinned. 'Back off and let us in a moment.'

'Sure,' Cade said, not really looking at him, his eyes on Dan Sheridan. 'You okay, Dan?'

'Fine,' Sheridan said. 'Angel here pitched in, gave me a hand.'

'That your name?' Howie Cade said, incredulity in his voice. 'Angel?'

'Would I lie about a thing like that?' Frank Angel asked him, keeping his face quite serious.

'Well shut my mouth,' Howie Cade said. 'Now I've heard everything.'

SIX

'Let me go with you,' Howie Cade said.

Dan Sheridan just looked at him. Then he looked at Frank Angel. He didn't say anything. They stood there in the middle of the jailhouse, Howie with the shotgun still cradled across his arm, a look of anguished entreaty in his eyes. Angel knew how he must feel: his need to redeem himself not only in Sheridan's eyes but also in the eyes of the whole town burned in Howie's expression. He leaned forward with the very eagerness of wanting it.

Sheridan shook his head.

'You better stay here and watch Burt,' he said.

'Dan!' Howie Cade said. There was deep hurt in his voice. 'Dan!'

'Listen, Howie,' Sheridan said, exasperation tinging his tone. 'I don't know how the hell many Flying H boys there are over the road, but there's sure as tomorrow half a dozen of them. I don't want—'

'To have a drunk on your hands,' Howie said. Sheridan started to speak but he held up a hand. 'It's all right, Dan,' he said. 'I guess you're right. I just thought after what happened down Fat Mary's, you'd maybe trust me to back you. No offence, Angel.'

'Sure,' Angel said.

'Give me that shotgun,' Sheridan said. 'I'm no damned use with a handgun at all.'

'Dan, let me go with you,' Howie said again, not looking at Sheridan.

Sheridan started to refuse but Angel spoke before he could.

'Why not?' he said. 'I can take care of Hugess for you.'

He was facing Sheridan, his back to Howie Cade, who

could not see the facial signals he was giving the Marshal. Sheridan caught the message and his eyebrows rose. Then he nodded, seeing what Angel had already seen, that Howie *needed* to go out there with him. He knew, and Angel knew he knew, that Howie might not be as effective at his side as Angel in the same place. But he had to have his crack at it.

'I better deputise you,' Sheridan said to Angel.

'No need,' Frank Angel said. He reached into the slit pocket inside his belt and drew out of it the silver badge with the screaming eagle. It caught the yellow light of the oil lamp hung from the ceiling and Sheridan stared at it as if it were a snake.

'Department of Justice?' he said. 'What the hell's that?'

'Accident,' Angel told him. 'I was just passing through. But it eases your problem some.'

Howie Cade's face had lit up like a Christmas tree.

'Oh, brother,' he said. 'Does it ever!' He slapped Sheridan on the back, his grin as wide as a slice of watermelon. 'Here's Larry Hugess lockin' the town up tight to stop us gettin' word out to the U.S. Marshal, and we got the Department of Justice right in here with us!'

Sheridan's eyes had lit up some, too. He looked pleased about something, like a man anticipating a good meal.

'Well,' he said. 'Well, well, well.'

'You think we can swing it?' Angel said.

'By God, Angel,' Sheridan said, his grin coming up full and warm, 'you just watch us do it!'

'All the luck you need,' Angel said as they started to move out.

'There ain't that much,' Howie said, but he was still grinning and Angel watched the two men as they walked across the street, dark against the brightly lit windows of the Palace Saloon. He could hear the tinny sound of someone playing a poorly-tuned piano inside. He watched Howie brace himself outside the batwings as Sheridan slid down the side of the saloon towards the back door.

'What the hell's goin' on out there?' shouted Burt Hugess from the cell in back. Angel kicked the door of the jail building shut and went around Sheridan's desk, taking a seat in the swivel chair.

'Nothing but bad news, Burt,' he replied finally. 'And all for you.'

The Palace wasn't anything like as palatial as its name implied. Johnny Gardner had fancied it up as best a man could in a building that was essentially a long, narrow box. The bar ran down the left hand side and curved in towards the left hand wall about three quarters of the way down the building. In the wide space at the end, there was a raised dais on which Harry Andrews, 'The Professor', tinkled endlessly with the jangly old piano. Tables and chairs were grouped in half-circled profusion between dais and bar, and on the right hand side of the building a wooden stairway led to a first floor balcony that ran all round the place like a minstrel gallery. There were rooms on both sides: some for the girls who worked in the saloon, others kept free for any of the Flying H boys who might be in town. The mahogany of the bar was highly shined, and ornately-carved fretwork frames held mirrors behind shelves behind bottles that caught amber light from the flaring coal-oil lamps that hung in a row down the center of the building. The floor was pine planking, scuffed and cut by a thousand sets of spurs; brass rail at the foot of the bar, brass cuspidors every yard. There was a chuckaluck layout and another for monte, at which Danny Johnston and a couple of the Flying H boys were sitting when Howie Cade came in through the batwings blinking in the bright light.

Gardner saw him first and his eyes went wide; he froze, the glass he had been polishing to a high shine held in his hands as if he was expecting someone to shoot it out of them. He looked at Howie Cade and Howie Cade looked right back at him, and then through him, quickly counting up the Flying H men in the place.

Johnston and three others at the monte table; Johnny Evans and Ken Finstatt at the bar. He couldn't see too clearly through the roiling smoke towards the back of the saloon and there wasn't any more time because Johnny Evans had spotted the saloonkeeper's rigid stance and followed his eyes. Now he nudged Finstatt and pointed at Howie with his chin, grinning. Danny Johnston looked up from his cards, saw Howie and smiled. His companions at the table stopped talking. They all smiled. 'Well, well, well,' Johnny Evans said softly. 'Look who's here.'

The Professor's background music petered out. He looked edgily at Johnny Gardner behind the bar, but Gardner wasn't moving. His eyes, like all eyes in the place, were on Howie Cade.

Howie was standing to one side of the batwings, his back against the wall. His gun was in its holster and he didn't look too well. He let his eyes move across the faces of all the men in the room, ignoring the contemptuous grins. He was looking for someone who might be wounded. None of them seemed to be. Then Sheridan slid in through the back door, almost but not entirely silently.

There was a collective sound in the room almost like the slow exhalation of a giant breath. Sheridan just stood there with the Greener across his forearm, waiting for Howie to open the ball. Howie opened it.

'Johnny,' he said. 'Very, very gently, reach under the bar and bring out that old riot gun you got hidden down there.'

Johnny Gardner didn't move, unless you could count the movement as his jaw dropped open as real activity.

'Do it, now, Johnny,' Howie said. His voice was still gentle, almost dreamy. But his hand had moved a couple of inches nearer to the holstered sixgun at his right hand side, and Johnny Gardner swallowed noisily. He ducked behind the bar and came up with his old sawn-off.

'On the bar, Johnny,' Howie said. 'But away from where the boys can get at it. Up here.' He gestured with his chin at the bar end nearest to himself.

'Yeah,' Johnny Evans said, his voice heavy, loud in the silence. 'And give the bum a drink while you're at it!'

Howie looked at Johnny Evans thoughtfully for a moment.

'Come here, Johnny,' he said, conversationally.

'Uh?' Evans was surprised.

'Do it,' came a voice from the back of the room. Sheridan hadn't moved, but his voice left no doubt in anyone's mind that the barrels of the Greener were presently pointing at Johnny Evans. Evans shuffled towards Howie, the grin still hanging on to his face.

'Unbuckle your gunbelt, Johnny,' Howie said.

He let Johnny Evans think about it, and about Sheridan back there with the shotgun. Evans unbuckled the belt and it thumped on the sawdusted boards.

'Making a habit of this,' Howie said, as if to himself. He didn't look like he had a fast move in him but the right hand flickered down and came up with the gun in it and he hit Johnny Evans across the side of the head, just above the ear. Every man in the saloon winced at the solid clunk the gun-barrel made. Johnny Evans went down on his knees as if in prayer before Howie, and Howie pushed him to one side. The Flying H man sprawled in the sawdust, and Howie kicked his boots.

'Nope,' he said, as if he'd been seeking something.

He turned to face the monte table where Danny Johnston was sitting.

'Danny,' he said gravely. 'Let me see you boys on your feet.'

He still had the gun in his hand; there was a fleck of blood on the barrel. Danny Johnston looked at the gun and then into Howie's face.

'Howie,' he said. 'Allus figgered you'd prob'ly go loco one day, an' now you've finally gone and done 'er. I'm proposin' us boys chip in an' buy you a va-cation in one o' them fancy rest-cure places they got back east in St. Lou. Whatcha say, boys?'

'Looks like he could use one,' the man on his right said.

'Funny, funn-y,' Howie Cade said. The backhand slap of the pistol barrel across the bridge of the man's nose was almost negligent, but everyone in the saloon heard the bones go as the man cartwheeled backwards over the table and hit the wall with a crash that shook the building. He slid down to the floor, his face a bright mask of blood, and Danny Johnston stared at Howie as if he'd just grown horns and a forked tail.

'You wouldn't, of course, have heard that someone tried to bushwack Sheridan down by the depot,' he said conversationally to Johnston. 'An' killed poor old Nathan Ridlow in the doing of it. Would you?'

'Uh . . .' Johnston said. The man on his left looked indignant.

'What the hell is this, anyway, Howie?' he growled.

'We want to talk to the man who came in here after Ridlow got it,' Howie said. 'He's probably got a hole in his hide someplace, too.'

'Well, sheet, Howie,' Danny Johnston said, placatingly, the colour back in his face now. 'Ain't nobody come in here a good half hour before you and the Marshal bust in here.'

'That's the truth,' his sidekick said. He was a tall, burly rider whom Howie recognised vaguely, having seen him around town a few times.

'You wouldn't know the truth if it bit you in the ass, Harvey,' he said conversationally. He moved maybe three inches nearer the Flying H rider, and the man paled, backing up.

'Howie,' he said hastily. 'You beat up on me, ain't nothin' I can do with Sheridan over there holdin' a scattergun on me. But you're off your cock if you think anybody come in here!'

'Who seen this guy come in here, anyway?' demanded Danny Johnston.

Howie just looked at him. Danny Johnston laughed in his face.

'Sheet, Howie. you really got the DTs this time. Johnny, maybe you better give Howie here a stiff drink afore he sees anythin' else!'

The jest was rough, but it was enough to take the cork out of the bottled tension of the saloon. The Flying H boys let loose. They laughed. Easy at first and then louder and louder until they were all hooting, slapping their legs, pointing at Howie.

Sheridan stood there and watched Howie taking it, watched him beginning to crumble. He looked as though he was shrinking inside his tattered clothes as the Flying H boys gave him the razzle-dazzle. And there wasn't a single solitary damned thing Dan Sheridan could do about it: Howie had to make the play, if there was going to be one.

The deputy stood there looking at his tormentors, hearing the racket of their jeers like the scorn of angels inside his head. He pleaded silently with Sheridan to step in, stop them; and knew that Sheridan would not move until he gave him some signal that he wanted him to. Howie could not do that, he could not finally show Sheridan that he had broken, and yet he knew that if they didn't stop jeering, if they didn't stop, he'd have to, have to . . . . . . his eyes shuttled sideways and fixed on the amber glitter of the bottles on the shelves behind Johnny Gardner. His shoulders slumped: my God, what I'd give for a drink, he thought.

Danny Johnston saw it all, and he grinned.

He fished into the fob pocket of his pants and slid out a silver dollar, which he flipped up in the air and then caught. Howie Cade looked at it.

'Here,' Johnston said, tossing it towards the deputy. 'Have a drink, bum!'

The dollar fell uncaught to the floor, spun on the boards,

lay still. Howie Cade looked at Danny Johnston and hate surged into his eyes and then died, stillborn. He looked at the dollar on the floor. There were tears in his eyes, tears of pure shame.

Sheridan cursed silently, knowing he would have to move now. He'd seen old fighting bulls pulled down by wolves, and knew they worked the same way the Flying H boys were working now. The baying pack, confusing the bull, taunting him, tiring him, exposing his lack of speed. The false attacks, the small snapping wounds. And then the moment when the old bull realised that all he could do was die, and something went out of him like a signal which the wiley wolves knew, recognised, sensed. Then they attacked in earnest.

Howie still stood there in the middle of the saloon with his head down and his eyes fixed on the floor. He looked up at Sheridan and Dan Sheridan's heart leaped. Whatever was in Howie's stance, it wasn't in his eyes any more. There was a fierce, exultant light in them.

'I don't feel good,' Howie mumbled, shielding his face from the Flying H riders. 'Maybe I will take a drink.'

He walked over to the bar, moving diagonally so that he was about in the center opposite the big mirror behind Johnny Gardner, who was reaching for the whiskey bottle when Howie moved.

So unexpected, so sudden was the explosion of action that nobody had a chance to even move. Howie had leaned forward on the bar and then he whirled around, the sixgun in his hand coming up and booming once, twice, three times, almost faster than you could count. He was poised like an athlete in a drawing, right knee slightly bent, right arm rigid with the sixgun smoking in it, eyes fixed on the second door in the quartet of them on the balcony above the saloon. There were two jagged holes in the wood of the door where Howie's slugs had blasted through the flimsy wood and the man who had been standing behind the door holding it ajar came out almost as if someone had shoved him from behind, bent forward as though he was going to butt some invisible foe in the belly, head on into the balustrade and over it in a splintering crash to land on one of the tables below. The table collapsed in a huge noise, men scrambling aside away from the spreadeagled body lying in the middle of the wreckage.

Very slowly, as though afraid to let out his breath too fast, Howie Cade straightened up. He looked at Dan Sheridan and Sheridan nodded. Howie went over and turned the dead man face up. He had never seen the man before. There were two bullet holes in the centre of the man's chest, one low on the right, the other higher on the left. There was also a raggedy bandage around the man's upper arm. It was soaked with fresh blood. There was straw clinging to the rough woollen shirt and caked horse manure on the man's boots.

'Anybody know this man's name?' Howie said. His voice was harsh. Nobody spoke.

'Looks like Hugess is importing cheap gunslingers by the dozen,' Howie said.

He went back across the saloon to where Danny Johnston and the tall rider called Harvey were still standing, eyes wide. While they watched him he punched the empty shells out of his sixgun and reloaded it, then deliberately, almost showily, put the gun back in the holster.

'Saw nobody come in, right?' he said musingly to Harvey.

Harvey said nothing, but his eyes moved right, left, right, looking for help which wasn't going to arrive.

Howie slapped the man's face. Not hard. Lightly, cuffing him almost affectionately.

'My, but you're a cheeky one,' he said, dreamily. Then his voice changed. 'You cross my path again in this town, Harvey, and I'll cut you down,' he snapped. '*Sabe?*'

The man nodded sullenly. Danny Johnston said nothing. Howie turned his attention towards the Flying H foreman. He picked up the whiskey that Johnston had been drinking.

'Now let me buy you a drink,' he said, and tossed the contents of the glass into Johnston's face. Johnston snorted and pawed at his face as the fiery liquid burned his eyes, cursing and spluttering as Howie Cade stepped back and let his fingers curl above the butt of the sixgun he had so showily holstered a few moments ago.

The message was plain and every man in the saloon held his breath. Danny Johnston pawed his eyes dry and looked at Howie. He looked at everyone else and then he shook his head.

'Un-hunh,' he said. 'Not me, Mary Ann.'

'Like I figgered,' Howie said, turning away with a sneer. 'Gutless.'

He turned his back completely on the Flying H man and looked over at Sheridan.

'Anything else?' he said, his head high, proud.

'Guns,' Sheridan reminded him.

'Oh, yeah,' Howie said. He looked at Johnny Gardner. 'Every Flying H man in the place, Johnny,' he told the saloonkeeper. 'Get his guns and bring them over to the jail.'

'Listen,' Gardener said. 'This ain't no fight of mine. I—'

'Get started,' Howie said, and there was a cold flatness in his voice that made Gardner jump. He came around the bar in a hurry and started lifting sixguns from the holsters of the Flying H boys.

'You know you're wastin' your time, Sheridan,' Danny Johnston said. '*We* can get more guns.'

Johnny Gardner had an armful of handguns. He looked at Sheridan.

'Over to the jail, Johnny,' Sheridan said. 'Leave them there.'

Howie Cade was eyeing Danny Johnston thoughtfully.

'Maybe we ought to make him put his hands on the bar,' he said, worlds of meaning in his voice. 'What do you say, Dan?'

Sheridan pursed his lips, as though thinking it over.

Danny Johnston's eyes got that nervous edgy look back in them. Small beads of cold sweat started out on his upper lip.

'It's a thought,' Sheridan said, letting Johnston sweat for a while. Then he shook his head. 'No. Not worth the effort.' He jerked the shotgun towards the doors. 'Get the hell out of town, Danny. Tell Hugess his plan backfired. Tell him next time not to send boys on a man's work.'

'I'll tell him,' Danny Johnston snapped, angrily. 'Don't you fret none.'

'Haul your freight!' Sheridan snapped back, patience running thin. He jerked the Greener again and Danny Johnston paled and backed off. That damned gun would blow a man clear into the next county. He headed out of the saloon with the Flying H boys trailing behind him and Sheridan and Howie Cade went to the door and watched them racket off down Front Street, raising a cloud of sifting dust that fell slowly back and down as the riders thundered across the railroad tracks.

'Damn fool grandstand play,' Sheridan muttered. He turned towards Howie Cade who was grinning at him. 'What the hell's so funny?'

'I was just going to say I'd buy you a drink,' Howie said.

Sheridan smiled. 'I reckon I'd enjoy one. Beer, Johnny!'

Johnny Gardner was just coming back from his errand to the jailhouse. He scuttled behind the bar, sweating from the exertion of carrying all that iron across the street on the double.

'Two beers, comin' up!' he echoed automatically.

Sheridan and his deputy clinked glasses and drank deeply, enjoying the cold chill of the liquid. Then the Marshal put his glass down and turned to face his deputy.

'Tell me just one thing,' he said. 'How the hell did you know that fellow was up there?'

'Hell,' Howie grinned. 'When I looked down at that dollar on the floor I seen a blob o' blood big as a dime, and another a few feet away and others that made a line goin' straight the stairs. There was only the one door open up there. He had to be behind it, watching everything.'

'You sure as hell took a long chance on that,' Sheridan said.

'Suppose so,' Howie admitted. 'Never occurred to me anyone else'd be up there.'

Sheridan shook his head in resignation. He didn't want to bring Howie down off his high; the deputy hadn't felt this good in a couple of years and it would be a poor friend who drew his attention to the odds against his having been right when he blasted away at that open door.

'You want another beer, Howie?' he asked.

Johnny Gardner bustled over as he heard Sheridan's words, anxious to be of service, rubbing his hands dry and reaching for the glasses. Howie Cade waved him away with a lordly gesture.

'Beer?' he said, scornfully. 'Beer? You think I want to spoil this feeling with *beer*? You got any champagne, Johnny?'

'He has,' Sheridan said, taking Howie's elbow and steering him towards the door. 'But you can't afford it on your pay!'

'Shucks, Dan,' Howie was saying as he got bum's-rushed through the batwings by the Marshal. 'I thought you were buyin'!'

Johnny Gardner watched them go with his mouth hanging open. They acted like men who didn't have a damned care in the world.

'Goddammed fools,' he snarled to the empty bar.

SEVEN

It was only a small sound.

Most men wouldn't have heard it, certainly men as deep in sleep as Angel had been before the sound was made. But Frank Angel wasn't most men. Long ago, when they'd first put him through all the punishing training courses of the Department in Washington, one of the things he'd been taught was to sleep with one ear cocked. They had a very simple way of teaching it, and once learned, the lesson was never forgotten. They worked him like a plowhorse all day and then when he collapsed, out like a light, in the barrack-like dormitory, they let him sleep. Somewhere between lights out and the grey death-light of pre-dawn, someone would eel into the room on soundless feet, and then, with a scream to wake the dead of an earlier century, empty a bucket of icy water on the naked belly of the sleeping man. After three or four times, a man started to listen, without knowing he was doing it, listening in his sleep for the soft slither of a foot on board, the slow creak of a quietly-opened door, the faint rustle of clothing when an arm is raised. He started to react fast, to come awake without the involuntary start with which most people awaken, without the need for the long seconds of focusing the eyes, alert and poised with one hand already on the sixgun beneath the pillow.

'Anyone's in your room while you're asleep sure as hell ain't there to gaze on yore fair white body,' the instructor had told him. 'By the time you find out why he is there, likely as not he'll have put a foot of steel in your belly. So when you know someone's there and where he's at – *move*!'

He came off the bed in a very fast, rolling movement, on his feet and crouched with the sixgun cocked and ready, whirling to face the figure by the door. She grinned.

'Well,' she said. 'And good morning to you!'

She was tall for a woman, Angel saw, five eight or nine at least and strongly, if slenderly, built. Her hair was a deep, burnished copper colour, and her eyes were as green as Spring grass. She wore a dark blue work shirt tucked into corduroy Levis, embroidered Indian moccasins on her feet. Her body was good. In fact, he realised, she was quite beautiful.

'Uh,' he said, lowering the gun and suddenly aware that he was bone naked.

If it bothered the woman she didn't show it.

'I'll get you some hot water to shave with,' she said tactfully and went out of the room before he could reply. He threw the sixgun on the bed and snatched for his pants, cursing softly under his breath. By the time she knocked on the door he was dressed. She came in and put the earthenware jug and bowl on the washstand. It had blue forget-me-nots on it. Steam spiralled upwards from the jug.

'I'm Sherry Hardin,' she said. Her voice was low-pitched, warm-toned. 'I own the hotel.'

'Glad to know you,' Angel said. 'Mind if I ask you a question? What—?'

'—was I doing in your room?' She smiled. 'Making sure you had a razor and stuff. Dan Sheridan said he wasn't sure whether you needed one and sent one of his over.'

'You weren't—'

'Here last night when Dan brought you in, I know,' she said. 'I was with Janet Mahoney – her husband owns the general store. One of her kids has whooping cough. I didn't get back until quite late. Is everything all right – the room, I mean?'

'Fine,' Angel said. 'By the way, where can I—'

'Get breakfast? Right downstairs. We've cooked you up something special. Heard how you helped out Dan Sheridan.'

'One other thing.'

'Yes?'

'You ever let anyone finish a sentence?'

She smiled. 'Not if I can help it. Dan's always telling me about that.'

'You think he's pretty special, don't you?'

She blushed slightly at his direct question but her eyes didn't shift away from his. She pushed back a straying lock of the copper hair from her forehead and smiled, almost challengingly.

'I'm very fond of Dan,' she said. 'He's like a brother to me.'

He didn't answer that one. When a woman tells a man that another man's like a brother to her, she's also telling him lots of other things.

'I'm going to get me a shave,' he said, rubbing a hand over his bristled jaw ruefully. 'Sure as hell need one.' She didn't take the hint.

'I'll watch,' she said, unabashed. 'I like to watch a man shaving. Gives me goose-bumps.'

He thought he'd better not reply to that one either. Sherry Hardin wasn't only a very beautiful woman, she also clearly didn't give a hoot in hell for what was commonly called convention. He unrolled the soft leather kit he always carried with him, containing a razor, shaving brush and soap, steel mirror, leather strop, stiff nail brush, soap, scissors, needles, thread, spare buttons, small ball of twine, all neatly packed away in pockets and loops on the flat leather square. For once, unexpectedly, he found himself feeling like a pernickety old maid and he asked her a question, working on the shaving soap with the brush to get a good lather.

'A little over seven years,' she said 'Hal and I came out here in the spring of '70.'

'Hal?'

'My husband. He died four years ago'

'I'm sorry.'

'No need to be,' she said. She gathered up her shoulders slightly, the movement not so much indicating that she didn't care about the subject as that she preferred not to dig up old bones, backtrack to the past.

'He wasn't . . . Hal never really liked this country,' she said quietly.

'But you do?'

'I love it,' she said, passionately. 'I love the space of it, the wildness. Or rather, I used to.'

'Until?'

He worked busily with the razor, keeping his eyes averted, not looking at her in the mirror over the washstand.

'Until lately,' she said, flatly. 'Believe it or not, this town used to be a pretty nice place to live. Kids playing in the street. Farmers coming in on weekends to do their shopping, gossip around. We had a produce market on Saturdays. Lots of people. Lots of laughter. Now . . . well, you've seen it.'

'What happened?' he asked.

'Larry Hugess happened is what happened,' she said. 'His hired thugs drove all the smaller farmers and ranchers out. One by one, they pulled stakes and moved on. Usually with a Flying H escort.'

'Didn't anybody put up a fight?'

'Oh, one or two. But it was no use. They couldn't face down hired guns – they weren't that sort of people. Hugess claimed they fenced off water his cattle needed. Eminent domain, he called it. First come, first served.'

'What about the Law?'

'The U.S. Marshal is in Winslow,' she said. 'That's around fifty-four miles away. Even if he was there on tap, waiting for us to call on him, which of course he isn't. He's got a pretty big bailiwick, Angel.'

'Frank,' he corrected her, thinking, yes, she was right. The U.S. Marshal patrolled an area that was about the size of Delaware. To do it he had the help of two deputies. That wasn't exactly what you'd call a deterrent to crime.

'How many men has Hugess got on his payroll?' he asked.

'Thirty, thirty-five,' she replied. 'It's hard to say – there are always some new faces coming in, others moving on.'

'Yeah,' Angel said. 'I met some of the boys. That Willie Johns. He's a mean one.'

'He is!' she said vehemently.

'Personal experience?'

She gave a theatrical shudder.

'Uhhhhh,' she went. 'He comes in here sometimes. Once he – he put his hands on me.' She tossed her bright hair as if getting rid of a dark thought.

'Now,' she said. 'How about some breakfast?'

'I could use some,' he said. 'Will you join me?'

'Pooh,' Sherry Hardin laughed. 'I had breakfast hours ago. But I'll sit and have some coffee with you.'

She turned and held the door open and he bowed to her with a smile and did one of those 'after you, Alphonse' gestures. She was very close and he could smell a faint, clean perfume. Her eyes were smiling as he looked down at her. He was standing near enough to feel the warm glow of her body and he stifled the sudden impulse to touch her. A quick light in her eyes told him that she had sensed his impulse and there was a quick lift of the corners of her mouth. Her lips were slightly parted, soft, warm. He pushed her shoulder.

'G'wan,' he said, mock-growling. 'I smell coffee.'

She ducked her head and went out into the corridor ahead of him. He couldn't see her face but he bet himself she was smiling, with perhaps a faint touch of triumph in the expression. She had a good walk and Angel watched the sensuous movement of her hips with pleasure. One of life's sheerest enjoyments was watching a healthy, beautiful woman walk. As if she sensed his gaze she turned her head and smiled impishly over her shoulder as she went down the stairs and into the dining room to the right at the foot of the staircase.

It was a bright, airy room with six or eight tables spread far enough apart so nobody would ever feel he was sharing his breakfast conversation with his neighbour. The tables were all circular, and each had a small glass jug with desert flowers in it. There was a big window with a square table up against it looking out on to the bustle of Front Street. They sat there and a tiny old Chinaman shuffled in with a platter of ham and eggs, bread, coffee, cream, sugar, and cups. He laid them all out without a word, working in neat, precise movements. Then he bowed just enough for it to be seen and went out without a word.

'Smells good,' Angel said, leaning over the food.

'It should,' she replied. 'I cooked it myself.'

Angel could see Dan Sheridan leaning against the hitchrail outside the jail down the street. The Marshal looked relaxed, comfortable. Angel got started on the food, asking the girl a question as he did.

'Two years come fall,' she told him.

'Tell me about him,' he pursued.

'Nothing much to tell,' she said. 'Dan had been kicking around since the end of the War, scouting for the Army, I think, hunting buffalo. I think he rode shotgun for Butterfields for a while, but I'm not sure if he told me that or I heard it someplace else. He just happened along at a time when the Flying H boys were getting a little too much for the town to handle. Jock Mahoney, Johnny Gardner, Jack Coltrane who runs the livery stable, some of the others hired him as town Marshal. You know the sort of thing: keep the town in line but don't stop the boys from spending their money.'

'I know the sort of thing.'

'I think the Flying H boys didn't mind. They kind of respected Dan. He never pushed them around. Just kept them from going too far.'

'Until the Burt Hugess thing.'

'Yes. Until then.'

'You think he made a mistake?'

'It could be,' she said, tonelessly. 'How's the food?'

'First class,' he said. 'You're a good cook.'

'I know. I make good coffee too.'

'Then pour me some.'

She poured more coffee and they sat in a comfortable, companionable silence while he finished his food. When he pushed the plate away and leaned back, she looked at him for a moment, as though uncertain what to say.

'Go ahead and ask,' he said, smiling.

'You're not supposed to be able to do that, Angel,' she said softly. 'Not quite so soon.' There was a breathlessness in her voice.

'Frank Angel,' he said. 'Twenty-seven years old. Born in Georgia, but I got most of my growth not far from here. Fort Dodge way. I work for the Government – I guess Dan told you that. And I'm on my way to Fort Griffin. That's about it.'

'The Justice Department,' she said. 'What does that mean?'

'Like I told Dan Sheridan,' he said. 'It's the Government Department that's responsible for all law-enforcement in the United States. My being here, however, is a pure accident.'

'You live in Washington?' she probed.

'Uh-huh.'

'With your parents?'

'No,' he said, softly. 'My parents died a long time ago.' There was a far-off glint of old anger deep in his eyes that made her regret her question. She filled the silence with another.

'Nope,' he grinned, his face boyish again. 'No wife. But I've got a beaut of a landlady. Her name's Mrs. Rissick.'

'Oh,' Sherry Hardin said. 'She's pretty?'

'Well,' Angel allowed, 'for a woman of sixty-eight, she's not bad. If you go for sixty-eight-year-old women.'

'And do you?' she asked with a straight face.

'Pour some more coffee,' he told her. They were smiling at each other like fools and they both realised it at the same moment, both knowing why. As the simultaneous thought occurred to them they laughed out loud.

'Aren't I the forward hussy, now,' Sherry Hardin said, almost to herself.

'Just pour the coffee in the cup this time,' Angel said, 'and tell me about Larry Hugess.'

She lifted the pot but didn't tilt it, and he looked at her, puzzled for a moment by the stiff shocked look on her face. She had gone pale beneath the warm tan and her eyes were fixed on the street outside. Angel turned quickly.

A phalanx of horsemen was coming down the street past the flat hulk of the warehouse behind the depot. In its van was a solidly built man in a dust-coated dark suit. At his right side rode Willie Johns and on the other Danny Johnston.

'No need,' Sherry Hardin said. 'No need now.'

And Larry Hugess led his men through the town like a king, along Front Street to the jail where Dan Sheridan stood waiting.

EIGHT

LARRY HUGESS came down Front Street as if he owned it.

Frank Angel came out on to the porch of the hotel to watch him go by and had to admit that Hugess was something to watch. He was a big man, broad across the shoulders, tall in the beautifully-tooled Denver saddle, head erect and eyes disdainful. Hugess was clad in a dark blue suit which, although dust-coated, was plainly tailor-made, as were the fine smooth leather boots he was wearing, glowing the way leather only glows from much and diligent polishing. If it hadn't been for the rig Hugess was using, Angel would have said he was a fine figure, but despite the fact that the grey Hugess was riding was a superb animal with the arched neck and graceful lines of an Arab, Angel noted that the man used a wicked-looking *chileno*, or ring bit. Any man who knew horses also knew that this kind of hardware was liable to break a horse's jaw if used too severely: it was the cruellest bit ever put into an animal's mouth and if Hugess had been a working cowman, nobody would have ridden alongside him. Angel noted too that Hugess spurned the lighter Texas or California-style saddle, burdening the animal with forty pounds and more of ornately tooled and silver-decorated leather and a three-quarter rig, topped off by the extra weight of an engraved Winchester carbine which Hugess patently didn't need to carry, since he had Willie Johns to guard one flank, Danny Johnston to take the other side, and four men to bring up the rear.

He rode easily, Larry Hugess, a man quite sure of himself and his dominion over this town. He had straight, heavy features, the face just beginning to jowl, the neck thick and obdurate. His eyes were shrewd and cool, assessing the mood of the street, the calculating intelligence behind them considering, weighing, accepting, rejecting.

It had pleased him to lift his blockade of the town, to remove his guards from the streets. In a way his action had been symbolic: he was telling Sheridan in so many words that it didn't matter whether he sent for the U.S. Marshal or not. It would take several days for any Federal law to get to Madison in enough force to set back Larry Hugess on his heels. By that time it wouldn't make any difference.

He weighed Sheridan's abilities contemplatively as he approached the jail. A good man; but slowed down to a walking pace by the injury to his gun hand. Still dangerous, though, as last night's events had shown. That had been a badly-botched business, but since no one but a few of his men had known the hired gun and the man had died without talking, no beans had been spilled. He had been very careful to make sure that the set-up was pulled by a stranger. But it had backfired; Sheridan and his deputy had run Danny Johnston and the boys out of town twice, which was a loss of face that must be redressed. The mood of the town was cowed, though, he noted: which meant that the lesson of Ridlow's death had not been lost on them. Sheridan would find no support among the townspeople. All he had was the drunk, Cade. Cade might have held together for the business last night. Hugess couldn't see him hanging on when the going got really hard. And he had decided, finally, that he was about to see that it did.

They were level with the Palace when Howie Cade stepped into the street. He had Sheridan's shotgun ported across his arm and he pointed it quite negligently at the oncoming riders. Hugess pulled his horse to a halt. Angel saw the animal throw its head as the wicked ring bit jarred its sensitive mouth.

'New bye-law in operation as of this ayem,' Howie said conversationally. 'You check your guns when you come into town.'

Hugess nodded, smiling. It came as no surprise to him at all that Sheridan had decided to defend by attacking. He had anticipated just such a demand, and his men were already under strict orders not to even consider using their guns except in extreme circumstances. Nevertheless, he couldn't help wondering about Cade. He surveyed the deputy contemptuously.

'You look like hell, Cade,' he said dispassionately.

Howie didn't rise. 'The guns,' he said again, gesturing with the shotgun.

'Suppose I say no?' Hugess said. 'You think you could get all of us with that?'

He curled his lip as he referred to the weapon Howie was holding.

'Be interestin' to see,' Howie said, settling slightly on his heels, his lips clamping into a thin line. He didn't look the slightest bit edgy, and his readiness to start in any time Larry Hugess opened the ball was so apparent that Hugess blinked, startled in spite of himself at the change in the man.

'Well, well,' he said softly. He turned to his men. 'All right,' he said.

Howie gestured with his chin towards the hitching rail outside the Palace. 'Hang your belts on there,' he said. 'Pick 'em up when you leave.'

Hugess smiled at the deputy's confidence: a patronising smile which didn't fail to have exactly the effect he intended. Howie Cade swung his eyes away from the big man, just that little spooked by Hugess. Hugess wasn't just some forty-and-found puncher on a lallyhoot, or even some paid gun. He was The Man, just about as powerful as they came. You messed with Larry Hugess at your peril, and here the sonofabitch was smiling at him like a cat who's contemplating some particularly juicy mouse he aims to eat up when he's good and ready. For some reason, it made him angry. He jerked the shotgun at Hugess who, despite his composure, reacted. Now it was Howie's turn to grin.

'I'll take that Winchester, too, Hugess,' he said.

Larry Hugess slid the weapon out of its saddle holster and handed it down. It was a pretty gun, the 1873 44-40 center-fire model. Its receiver and breech were custom-engraved to Hugess' own specification, an ornate pattern of leaves and flowers decorating the flat surfaces. Howie would have given a year's pay for a gun like it, and it showed in his eyes.

Hugess smiled to himself: he had always believed that any man – and therefore every man – could be bought. Not necessarily with money, of course. Some men you bought with gold; others women; still others power. He had just established Howie's price and he filed the information away, not knowing how totally wrong he was.

'Marshal,' he said, cordially, moving his horse across Texas Street to the rail outside the jailhouse. 'Good morning.'

Sheridan nodded. He'd taken in the whole procession, watching to make sure that Larry Hugess wasn't planning a strike at the jail, with some of his guns hidden away in an alley to cut down the Marshal and his deputy and spring Burt Hugess. In some ways he was surprised Hugess hadn't done just that and he couldn't figure why. Maybe he'd find out now.

'Been expecting you,' he said.

'Like to talk,' Hugess said. 'Maybe see Burt.'

'Fine with me,' Sheridan said. If he noticed that Angel was on the porch of the Oriental Saloon, directly across the street, he didn't show it by either word or movement.

Hugess swung down from the saddle, and his riders started to follow suit. Sheridan stopped them with a word. They looked at Hugess, and Hugess looked at Sheridan.

'You visiting your brother's fine,' Sheridan said. 'He's not their brother.'

Willie Johns kneed his horse forward, crowding Sheridan back on the porch. He looked so tense, so anxious to start something that Howie Cade started to move from his post across the street where he was keeping the Greener pointed in the general direction of Hugess' men.

'How about I teach yore Marshal some manners, Mr. Hugess?' Johns hissed.

Hugess ignored the threatening pose, the ugly words.

'Go across and wait for me in the Palace,' he said to Johns. 'Keep out of trouble.'

Willie Johns looked at Hugess, only just succeeding in keeping the sneer off his face. He reined his horse around angrily, almost knocking Howie Cade over. Johns had blood in his eye and everyone there knew he was liable to go off like a stick of dynamite if anyone sparked him, so Howie said nothing, just stood and watched as the Flying H boys trooped into the cool depths of the Palace. He stayed on the porch of the jail as Hugess went into the office with Dan Sheridan. Angel stayed where he was too. He looked towards the Hotel longingly. Maybe he could get a cup of coffee later. Sherry Hardin, he thought, remembering the colour of her hair and the look in her eyes.

Inside the jail, Dan Sheridan was opening up the cell and Larry Hugess was covertly checking over the strength of the building. Solid and squat, it would be a bastard to take against determined men who were well-armed and had plenty of ammunition and water. A frontal attack was out, then, unless there was no other way. It might come to that yet.

'Hey, Larry,' Burt Hugess was saying, grinning hugely. 'I figured it was about time you come to bail me out. This place's beginning to stink.'

It was clear that any thought other than that his release was immediately imminent had not crossed his mind. Larry had always bailed him out. Larry would do it now. Larry could always fix everything. He'd think of something – he always did.

Larry Hugess looked at his younger brother, not understanding why he gave a damn about him and knowing all the same that he loved him, and needed to protect and care for him even though Burt was a wastrel, a womaniser, and worse – a killer whose actions had several times endangered Larry's own ambitions and come perilously close to dragging the Hugess name into the dirt. He loved his brother as he loved no other human being, and he did not know why, but it was a love tempered by an anger that made him want now to shake Burt the way a terrier shakes a rat, to slap him like a wayward child, to chastise him for the stupidity that had led him to kill – of all people – the harmless Clell Black, a man who had never willingly hurt a soul in all of his thirty-odd years of life. He wanted to tell Burt that he, Larry, had broken his back working for the power and the wealth that he now had, while Burt had never done a thing. He wanted to make Burt understand that his deliverance would only be effected at the cost of stopping all work at the ranch, of hiring expensive – and unreliable – gunmen, of running up against a man who, to be truthful, Larry Hugess respected – Dan Sheridan – and the very law he represented. And all because in a stupid drunken killing rage, Burt had lost control. This was the worst thing of all to Larry Hugess. A strong man never lost control of himself. He was proud that he had never done so. Never.

To tell the truth, he thought, he ought to let his brother rot in jail. If it had been some other cause, he might even have done so. But for murder Sheridan would see Burt hanged, and Larry Hugess was not about to stand still while his brother was hanged at Winslow where the whole damned Territory could see the Hugess name on the front pages of the *Enterprise*. So there was only one thing he could do.

Sheridan was waiting for him to speak. Burt was looking at both of them like a dog who's heard the word 'walk' – he couldn't wait to get out.

'Well, Burt,' Larry Hugess said.

'Come on, Larry, come on, come on,' Burt said. 'Open this damned door, Sheridan.'

When nobody moved, his face fell, as though someone had

told him there was no Santa Claus. 'Hey,' he said plaintively. 'What is this? Do I get out or don't I?'

'As to that,' Hugess said levelly, 'perhaps Marshal Sheridan and I could discuss it.'

Sheridan laid it down flat and hard. 'No discussions, Hugess.'

Larry Hugess let a frown touch his forehead. He let his cold grey eyes rest on Sheridan's. They both knew what he wasn't saying: in effect, he was inviting Sheridan to back down, no harm done. Or take the consequences.

'No deals, no discussions, no fix, nothing, Hugess!' Sheridan said. 'Your brother is going to Winslow and he's going to be tried.'

'Now,' Hugess said. 'Let's not be hasty, Marshal.'

'Hasty, hell!' Sheridan snapped. 'You've been high man on the totem pole so long you think all you got to do is snap your fingers and everyone jumps, Hugess. Your little brother here killed a man in cold blood and you figure you can ride into town and get him off the hook. You figure you've got it all tied up with a string. But you're wrong. I'm going to take Burt out of here and I'm going to ride him across to Winslow and there's not a solitary damned thing you can do about it!'

Larry Hugess felt the anger rising in him like mercury in a thermometer.

'You talk a good fight, Sheridan,' he snapped, coldly. 'You forgotten you have to cross Flying H land to get to Winslow?'

'I haven't forgotten,' Sheridan said.

'Go on, Larry,' Burt urged. 'Lay it on him.'

'Shut up, Burt,' Larry Hugess said, without emphasis. Burt Hugess closed his face with a snap like a clam, and Sheridan permitted himself a grin.

'You're being valued, Burt,' he said. 'Your big brother's just working out how much it's going to cost him to spring you, if he tries. And wondering whether it's worth it. Right, Hugess?'

Larry Hugess looked at him with hooded eyes. Sheridan was too confident and he couldn't figure out why.

'You won't make it,' Hugess said, softly, letting the warning finally come out.

'Wrong,' Sheridan said. 'We'll make it. Your ace has been trumped, Hugess. You can lean on me all you like. I doubt you'll make the mistake of trying it on the U.S. Department of Justice.'

'What the hell does that mean?' snarled Hugess.

Sheridan grinned. He was enjoying Hugess' discomfort, and now he laid it on thick and heavy, relishing the way the big man's face fell as he gave it to him.

'We were planning to get word to the U.S. Marshal,' Sheridan said. 'You put that one out of the window by blockading the town.'

'So?'

'You shouldn't have done it, Larry,' Sheridan said. 'If there'd been no blockade he'd have left town and you'd have had me. As it is, he didn't, and I've got you.'

'What are you jabbering about?' Hugess snapped, patience at an end. 'Who's "he"?'

'Burt and me got ourselves a guardian Angel,' Sheridan explained. 'Frank Angel. Special Investigator of the Department of Justice. He's the man your boys stopped from leaving town. He's riding with me and Howie and Burt across to Winslow.'

Burt looked from Sheridan's triumphant face to the crestfallen one of his brother. 'Larry?' he said. 'What you goin' to do, Larry?'

Larry Hugess was shaken, but nothing showed on his face even though his mind was racing. Damn the luck! To have a Justice Department investigator happen into town at this moment was nothing but the purest bad luck. However, Dan Sheridan was counting his chickens a sight too early. Frank

Angel had no means of contacting his superiors. Ergo, they did not know exactly where he was. So if he was alone . . .?

'Angel, eh?' he said. 'You got lucky, Sheridan.'

'You might say,' Sheridan smiled.

'Larry?' Burt said, desperately. 'What you goin' to do?'

Larry Hugess turned to face his brother, spreading his hands in a theatrical shrug. He kept his voice quite without inflexion.

'Can't do a damned thing, kid,' he said. 'You got Federal law watching over you and I can't buck that. The Marshal here will take you over to Winslow and – well, you'll just have to hold on, Burt. I'll get you the best damned lawyer in the Territory, you know that—'

'Larry?' Burt Hugess' voice was disbelieving. It was as if he had seen Dan Sheridan actually move a mountain. 'You gonna let them take me?'

'I don't see what the hell else I can do,' Larry Hugess said. He looked at Sheridan and nodded at the door. Sheridan unlocked it and bowed him through ironically. Burt Hugess watched his brother go with his mouth hanging open. Larry Hugess didn't even look back.

'All right, Sheridan,' he said, 'I see how things are.'

'Just one more thing,' Sheridan said.

Hugess stopped at the rail dividing the office.

'You make the mistake of trying to take your brother away from us,' Sheridan said levelly, 'and he's liable to get accidentally dead. You read me?'

Larry Hugess nodded. It was worth swallowing the insults, letting the Marshal have his moment of triumph. He had learned what he needed to know. Sheridan had now become a secondary priority. He went out into the sunlit street. Howie Cade was outside the door. He turned and looked at Hugess.

'Get what you came for?' he said.

Larry Hugess went past him and across the street without speaking. There was no emotion in him now, just cold determination. He had discovered what his course of action must be, and he was now going to put the wheels in motion. He neither knew now or cared whether the dust he'd thrown in Sheridan's eyes had been effective or not. Larry Hugess had not become the most powerful man in this region by worrying about trifles like that. He preferred to use legal methods where legal methods would work and he preferred not to step outside the law unless it was absolutely necessary. But he had amassed power so that he could use it, the way another man will use a hoe or an axe. When it was necessary, he would employ all of it. Like now.

He walked into the Palace and his men looked up expectantly. Johnny Gardner hurried along the bar with a spotless glass and Larry Hugess' favourite brand of bourbon whiskey.

'Everything jake?' Danny Johnston asked.

'Let's get a table,' Hugess replied, as Johnny Gardner hovered nearby. 'Willie, you want to join us?'

Willie Johns nodded and slouched across to the table, where Larry Hugess poured him a drink. Hugess did not look at the gunslinger as he spoke.

'There's a man in town called Angel,' he said, softly. 'Frank Angel. He's an Investigator for the Department of Justice.'

'The—'

'Quiet, damn you!' hissed Hugess as Danny Johnston started to speak. 'That's right, the Department of Justice.'

'Federal law,' mused Willie Johns. 'That ups the ante a mite, don't it?'

'How the hell did he happen along?' Johnston wanted to know.

'It makes no damned difference how,' Hugess told him. 'All that matters is that he's here and he's going to back Sheridan. They plan to take Burt across to Winslow for trial. I plan to see they don't.'

The two men looked at him. His florid face was set in a heavy frown of determination and they felt an almost tangible aura coming from him, a sense of something black and evil set in motion and out of control.

'Listen, Boss,' Danny Johnston said, nervously. 'That's heavy stuff . . .'

'You think I'm going to let them take my brother out and hang him?' hissed Larry Hugess, controlling his urge to shout, hands flexing on the table in front of him like the huge paws of some carnivorous beast. 'You think I'm going to stand by while they drag my name through the dirt? Everything I've built shot to hell by some snivelling snooper? Not by a long chalk! By God, not by a long chalk!'

Danny Johnston looked at Willie Johns and Willie Johns grinned.

'What do you want done, Mr. Hugess?' Willie Johns asked softly.

'Angel!' Hugess ground out. 'This Frank Angel. I want him found. I want him found fast. And then I want him – dead!'

'Quiet?' Johns asked, his voice still feather light and gentle. 'Or noisy?'

'It doesn't matter a damn!' Hugess said. 'Quiet would be better, but I don't care how you do it. Just wait until I can get back to the Flying H, then get started. Hunt Angel out of wherever he's hiding. Then kill him!'

NINE

LARRY HUGESS rode out of Madison soon after midday.

By that time, Dan Sheridan and Howie Cade had told Angel everything that had transpired in the jailhouse while Hugess was there. The three of them sat there now, nursing tin cups of coffee. Sheridan's face was reflective, as was Angel's. Only Howie Cade was jubilant, high on the way they'd faced down Hugess and his men.

'And now he's headin' back to the Flyin' H with his tail atween his legs,' Howie grinned.

'I'm not so sure,' Sheridan said.

'Hell, I just seen him leave!' Howie said.

'About his tail,' Sheridan explained. 'He backed down a sight too easy for my liking. Not Larry Hugess' way at all.'

'Hellndamnation, Dan,' Howie Cade said. 'You're a gloomy bastard.'

'Yup,' Sheridan said.

'What you figure his next move to be?' Angel asked him.

'He'll wait for us to move,' Sheridan said. 'I think.'

'You don't figure he'll make a frontal attack on the jail?'

'Can't see it,' Sheridan replied. 'He knows two men could hold this place against a small army. It's built like a fort.'

Angel nodded, his own thoughts busy. From what Sheridan had told him of Hugess' reactions, he didn't think the rancher was going to wait for the Marshal to make a move. Hugess wasn't that kind of man. He'd grab the bull by the horns and throw it into the next field, but he wouldn't sit around waiting to see what the bull was going to do. Hugess was strong, cunning, intelligent and powerful. Angel had his own ideas about the Flying H man's possible course of action.

'A suggestion,' he said. Sheridan looked up, eyebrows raised politely.

'You and Howie cover each other the whole time from now on,' Angel said. 'One doesn't go out in the street without the other covering. Or I'll cover both of you.'

Sheridan looked at the Justice Department man without saying anything. His eyes dropped to the gun at Angel's hip.

'When did you put that on?' he asked quietly.

'When you deputised me,' Angel smiled.

Sheridan nodded, and the silence grew.

'Hey, what the hell is this, a secret society?' Howie Cade crowed.

Angel didn't answer him. Dan Sheridan just looked up at Howie and then the light dawned in the deputy's eyes and he sat down.

'Oh,' he said. 'I get it now.'

It had taken them both a little longer to put it together but only a little. Given that Hugess couldn't take his brother out of the jail without a bad fight; given that he couldn't sit around waiting for them to take Burt across to Winslow to be tried; there was only one other thing he could do.

'He aims to take us out one by one,' Howie said.

'That's right,' Angel said. 'And my guess is the first one he'll go after will be me.'

'Willie Johns,' Howie said.

'What about him?' Sheridan asked.

'When Hugess rode out of town, he took Danny Johnston and the rest of his boys with him,' Howie said. 'Everybody except—'

'Willie Johns,' Angel said softly.

Both men looked at him. Willie Johns was the fastest man with a gun either of them had ever seen. He was sudden death and they knew it and they knew Angel knew it. But Dan Sheridan couldn't suggest Angel back away from the man. Every instinct told him he ought to tell Angel to get on his horse and get the hell out of Madison, that this fight was none of his making and there was no point in getting killed for a town he'd never heard of before two days ago. But the words wouldn't come, and so he just hung his head, not looking at Angel as the Justice Department man got up from the chair and put the tin cup down on the scarred old desk.

'Jesus, Angel,' Howie Cade said. 'Listen, I'll come with you.'

'We both will,' Dan Sheridan said, starting to get up, but Angel stopped both of them with an upraised hand. Sheridan stopped, halfway from the seat of the chair, eyebrows knitting in puzzlement.

'Got an idea,' Angel said.

Howie Cade snorted. 'You'll need better than that if you aim to go against Willie Johns, Angel. Here, take the Greener an'—'

Angel shook his head.

'He sees me with that thing, he'll hunt cover and wait,' he said. 'Or Hugess will have one of his boys try for me from ambush. Willie Johns will try to pick a quarrel with me and make me use my gun. Then he'll have a perfect excuse for blowing me apart.'

'So?'

'So maybe I'll surprise him,' Angel said, and he was out of the door before either of them could speak again. Sheridan lunged to his feet, heading after the Justice Department man; in the same instant Howie Cade did the same thing, and they collided like two comics in a slapstick routine, cursing at each other wordlessly as they pushed apart and went out after Angel into the bright noon sunshine. He was already across the street. They saw him push through the batwing doors of the Palace like a man without a care in the world.

Willie Johns was into his fourth game of solitaire when Angel came in through the door. Johnny Gardner was the only other person in the place, and the sound he made when he managed to swallow the ball of fright in his throat sounded like someone pulling a boot out of a mudhole. His eyes rolled heavenwards as if praying for some sweet chariot to swing low and carry him home, then skittered slanchwise to watch Willie Johns, who was weighing Angel with eyes as friendly as those of a hungry sidewinder.

'OmiGod,' Gardner managed. The sound of his voice hung in the still, damp air like a fragile bird. He watched Angel walk straight along the bar, his left hand touching it lightly as if for balance, until he was close to Willie Johns.

Willie watched him come. He had his guns on, and he knew this had to be his man. Nobody else in town but himself and Sheridan, and if you cared to count him Howie Cade, was wearing a gun. The stranger had on a gun: ergo, he was Angel. He'd seen him before.

'Well, well, well,' Willie Johns said. This was the cowboy who'd backed off at the bridge when they'd closed up the town. The knowledge spread inside Willie like warm honey. This was going to be a pushover.

Angel was not more than about twelve feet away now, and Willie moved his hands slightly, drawing Angel's attention to the guns in their curiously-canted holsters at his sides. As if it had been a signal, Angel stopped. Willie allowed himself a little smile.

'I see you're wearing your guns, Willie,' Angel said.

Willie nodded. He was curious to see how Angel would play this.

'It's not allowed any more,' Angel said mildly.

'Don't aim to take 'em off,' Willie said. 'What you figger to do about it?'

Angel stood at the bar, head canted very slightly to one side as though debating that very point in his mind. What he was actually doing was very carefully assessing Willie Johns' position in the chair and the position of the chair in relation to the table. He was ready for Willie. He had been ready ever since he had left the jail and crossed the street, using that small piece of time to discipline his mind and body in the way that the little Korean, Kee Lai, had taught him during his training in the echoing gymnasium in Washington*. The deep inner reserves of self which the Chinese call *ch'i* can be summoned at will with training, to bring all of the self, all of the power of the mind and the body together into one place for one moment of time, a combination infinitely stronger than the separated sum of the two. He was ready and he moved.

Angel took three steps and Willie Johns reacted as Angel had expected. He kicked his chair back away from the table and went for the guns at his side and as they both moved Angel shouted *'Sheridan!'*

Willie Johns wore his guns in their peculiar hang because, given that he could set himself into the almost-deformed crouch that went with the fast-draw technique he had perfected, the guns lay almost horizontal to the ground. All that he had to do was slide them back seven inches and they were ready to fire, a method infinitely faster than the long down-and-up-and-level-and-fire technique most men used with the sixgun. Angel knew all about that kind of technique, and he also knew its disadvantage: that you had to be set just so, flat on your feet and able to swivel the body through perhaps forty degrees from right to left or left to right to facilitate the pulling of the gun. Willie had been none of these and in addition, Angel had shouted the name of the Marshal, causing in Johns that millisecond of indecision, that instant of fear that he had been whipsawed, which made him scrabble for his guns instead of the clean, fast, unbeatable draw that he would otherwise have made. Even so, Willie Johns was fast: incredibly fast. He would still have killed nine men out of ten put up against him. But not Frank Angel.

Frank Angel was fast too, and his sixgun thundered a fractional fatal fragment of a second ahead of the gunman's weapons. Both of Willie's guns exploded wildly, the trig-

* Related in *Trap Angel*

gers jerked by reflex action as Angel's unerring bullet hit him about an inch to the right of the median line of his forehead and half that distance above the left eyebrow. It lifted Johns off his feet and hurled him backwards as if he had been swatted by some enormous invisible giant wielding a bat, smashing Johns across the room and against the wall of the saloon, with a crash that set bottles rattling on Johnny Gardner's shelves. The saloonkeeper watched, his mouth a wide 'O' as Willie Johns slid down the wall like a broken doll, leaving a thick smear of something oozing in a long half-circle on the painted surface before falling sideways into the clotted sawdust.

'Je-zuss,' Gardner whispered. He'd kept saloons in a lot of hard towns, seen plenty of tough men fight. But never anything like this, never. He let out the breath he hadn't known he was holding in a long quavering sigh as Dan Sheridan and Howie Cade burst in through the batwings, guns up. They looked at Angel and they looked at what was left of Willie Johns. There was a lot of blood now.

'Frank!' Sheridan said, coming across the saloon. 'You all right?'

Angel frowned slightly and then the light came back into his eyes. It was as if some part of his soul had gone to a far place, and Sheridan recognised what it was and waited, just putting his hand on Angel's shoulder.

'Fine,' Angel said, pasting on a smile that he didn't think fitted too damned well.

Howie Cade was shoo'ing people away from the batwings. They all wanted to come in now and see what had happened.

'A question,' Angel said to Sheridan.

'Shoot.'

'Who's guarding Burt Hugess?' Angel asked.

Howie Cade heard what he said, and he spat out a disgusted curse. He shoved his way through the people on the boardwalk outside and ran across the street, every line of him showing his own self-disgust. Angel's smile changed from a forced to a genuine one. He looked at Sheridan who nodded and then turned with him towards the door.

'Here,' Johnny Gardner said, coming to the end of the bar. 'Here, what am I supposed to do with him?'

He jerked his head at the sprawled body of Willie Johns. Angel nodded and pursed his lips as though debating Gardner's question deeply. Then his face cleared and he looked up.

'Why don't you have him stuffed?' he said.

TEN

HOWIE CADE stood in front of the long mirror in the Hardin House and scowled at his reflection. Damned if he didn't look like a meal-ticket Indian on a run-down reservation. His eyes were red-rimmed, bloodshot. He had something that might have been a long stubble or a short beard, but wasn't either: he couldn't recall the last time he'd had a proper shave or for that matter put saddle soap or polish anywhere near his boots, which were cracked and down-at-heel. Jesus, he thought, I need a bath.

'Sherry?' he said.

Sherry Hardin looked up from the table at the window where she was sitting watching Frank Angel make a hole in the meal she'd cooked for him and Howie. They sat at the window so that Angel could keep an eye on the jail while Sheridan was in there alone with Burt.

Later, Sheridan would come eat, changing places with Angel. Howie would be cover for both of them.

'You ever cut a man's hair?' Howie asked, and Sherry grinned.

'Once or twice,' she said. 'Once or twice.'

'I hate to ask you this,' Howie said.

Sherry looked at Angel and Angel grinned.

'He sure as hell needs all the help he can get,' Angel said. 'He's no oil painting and that's for sure.'

'The wreck of the schooner *Hesperus* would be more like it,' the girl said. 'Sit down in that chair, Howie.'

'That chair?' Howie said.

'Don't hedge,' Sherry told him. 'You want a shave and a haircut. I'm going to give you one.'

'Listen,' Howie said, nervously. 'I was thinking maybe

I'd leave it for now. You know. Do it later. Tomorrow, maybe.'

'Sit there,' Sherry said firmly. She led him to the chair, put her hands on his shoulders and pushed him into it. Then she rummaged in a drawer and came up with some long-bladed scissors.

'Listen, Sherry,' Howie said. 'Angel, listen.'

'Quiet,' the girl mock-growled, and started in on his greasy locks. She held her lower lip in her teeth as she concentrated and Angel watched her working, enjoying the movements of her body and how she was taking the job so seriously. Howie sat like a circus elephant as she cropped away, pausing only once to bang on the wall and shout to the Chinaman back there to fill a bath with hot water *pronto*. Howie opened his mouth to protest, thought better of it, closed it again and set his face like a bear-trap. His expression was that of a man who'd ought to have known better in the first place than to put himself in the hands of a woman.

'You know, Howie,' Sherry said, judiciously squinting at the results of her handiwork, 'that's not a half-bad face you had hidden under all that foliage.'

'Arrrgh,' Howie said, turning bright pink.

'Bath leddy,' the Chinaman said, poking his head around the doorway of the kitchen.

'Off you go, my boy,' Sherry told Howie, slapping him into action. 'Be good and scrub your neck now. And give me a call if you want your back rubbed.'

'Aw, hell, Sherry,' Howie said. He didn't know where the devil to put his expression, so he pasted on a scowl and stumbled out into the kitchen. Sherry Hardin turned towards Angel, who had gotten up from the table and was strapping on his gunbelt preparatory to going out into the street. She put her hand gently on his arm.

'You want me to wait for him?' he grinned.

'No,' she said softly. Her coppery hair caught the sunlight from the window. 'Howie's all right. I'll find him some of

Hal's clothes: they were about the same size. He'll be fine. It's you I'm worried about. I heard about Willie Johns.'

'Howie should learn to keep his tall tales to himself,' Frank Angel said. 'Scaring children like that.'

'Children yourself!' she reacted. "I'm not a child, Angel. Never think that.'

They looked at each other for a long moment and he sighed.

'Lady,' he said. 'Haul off.'

They both smiled together. Sherry Hardin put a finger against his chest.

'I'll get you yet,' she said.

'Who's running?' he replied.

He got his hat and went towards the door. She came with him and laid the same gentle-touching hand on his forearm again.

'I know,' he said. 'I'll take care.'

She put on a look of mock-exasperation.

'Will you quit reading my mind, sir?'

'Deal,' he said. 'As long as you never try reading mine.'

He went out into the street and she watched him go, a tall, confident man, assured, self-contained. For some reason the sight made her sad and she tossed her head in that special way she had, turning on her heel and hurrying upstairs to find Howie Cade some clean clothes.

If anything was bothering her by the time Dan Sheridan came across to eat his dinner, it wasn't showing on her face.

When Sheridan came back to the jail, Angel was sitting at the smaller desk with his sixgun disassembled on the flat top in front of him and his fingers smeared with cleaning oil. He'd taken another gun down from the rack and put it in his holster. He didn't plan to be the first Department of Justice troubleshooter to go into the big black book they kept at Headquarters with the epitaph 'Died while cleaning his gun'.

'Where's Howie?' Angel asked.

'He'll be right along,' Sheridan said. 'He just had to take one sashay through town in his new outfit.' He shook his head. 'I couldn't believe my eyes,' he confessed. 'He looked like the old Howie again.'

'You give him his guns?'

'Yep,' Sheridan nodded.

'That was a nice thing you did, Dan,' Angel said. Sheridan had told him he had Howie's guns. He'd hocked them to Johnny Gardner for booze a long time back. Sheridan had paid Howie's tab and redeemed the guns. He'd showed them to Angel: a *buscadero* belt with two fitted holsters, the fine soft leather cut, tailored for one man and one man only. The twin, ivory-handled Peacemakers had consecutive serial numbers and showed all the signs of good care and sensible use. There wasn't so much as a tiny pit on the metal, and the chambers had clicked softly and smoothly when he rolled them on the palm of his hand with the hammer on the second notch. Sheridan had taken them over to the Hardin House when he went for his meal and handed them without comment to his deputy. Howie had taken the belt and guns out of Sheridan's hands with the care a new mother accepts her baby from the doctor, the same light of wonder shining in his eyes.

'Hey,' he had said, softly. 'Hey, Dan.'

Nobody looked at him while he blinked and sniffed around, shuffling his feet, ducking his head, getting hold of it all. Then he strapped the gunbelt on. He looked like something now. He had on an old shirt of Hal Hardin's, faded blue, but still in good condition; dark trousers with a faint pin stripe in them. Even the boots Sherry had found had turned out to be a good fit. The only thing Howie was shy was a hat, and he'd told Dan he was going to go across to Mahoney's and get himself one on the way back to the jailhouse.

Sheridan went on ahead down the street, while Howie got

himself just so in front of the long mirror he'd used earlier. When he was all set, Sherry took his face in her hands and planted a kiss on his surprised face. Howie managed to fire off a four-alarm blush and stumbled out of the Hardin House into the street, a grin plastered across his face about half as wide as the Cimarron River. He still had it on when the three men jumped him from the alley alongside the Oriental.

It was very smooth, very neat, very quick.

A man Howie had never seen before stood in his path as he came off the sidewalk to cross the alley. The man was tall, gangling. Howie noted the prominent Adam's apple and the scrawny throat like a turkey-cock's.

'Howie,' the man said. 'You got a minnit?'

Howie frowned momentarily but he was feeling too good with the world to react the way he should have done. He stopped to talk to the man and as he did the rope that had been covered with sand and dust, and into whose loop he had stepped was pulled, and he went down into the dirt with a thud that jarred the breath out of his body. Cursing, spluttering to get the dust out of his mouth, Howie clawed for the guns at his side and as he did the man on the horse kicked the animal into a jumping run. The rope tightened with a twang and Howie's body was whipped off the ground and then hit it bouncing, jarring him almost unconscious, rolling him in front of a doorway in which stood the shadowed form of Danny Johnston. Johnston stepped out of concealment, his arm rose and fell, and the drawn sixgun in his hand glinted in the sunlight. The barrel slammed against the unprotected head of the deputy, who had scrabbled to one knee, flattening him face down in the dust. When Howie tried once more to get off the ground, Danny Johnston's arm rose and fell again.

This time Howie went down and stayed there, blood trickling quietly from the gash in his scalp into the heedless ground.

They dragged the unconscious form into a tumbledown

wooden hut that stood at the rear of the Oriental and somewhat to the north on open ground that stretched across to the broken edges of the bluffs above Cat Creek. When they had him out of sight they stripped him of his new clothes; Johnny Evans, the rider who'd done the roping, was about Howie's size, and he pulled them on.

When he was ready, he slid Howie's guns out of their tooled leather holsters, and checked them. Both had five shells in the chambers, and Johnny Evans cocked one of them and pointed it at Howie Cade's unconscious head. Danny Johnston stopped him with a cursed command. 'Put that away, you goddamned fool,' he snapped. 'You want to queer the whole deal?'

Johnny Evans nodded slowly, once, twice, three times, drawing in his breath deeply. 'Later,' he promised. 'I owe him.'

'All right, later,' Johnston said, his temper short. 'Later.'

He checked the door: there wasn't a human being in sight. He could see Nate Ridlow's wagons still parked in their neat row in the corral behind Mahoney's. A woman was crossing the bridge on Texas with a shopping basket in her hand. The sagebrush-speckled flat between where Johnston stood and the creek was deserted.

'Let's go,' he said. 'He trussed good?'

'Like a turkey,' the third man, the one with the Adam's apple told him.

'*Bueno*,' said Johnston.

They went out of there and down the alley to the street. They crossed without haste and went into the livery stable. Their horses were there. Nobody took any notice of them. It was three o'clock.

'Where the hell *is* he?'

Dan Sheridan's voice wasn't so much worried as exasperated.

Angel got to his feet. He'd had time to put the sixgun back together without hurrying, which meant Howie had been at least ten, maybe even fifteen minutes. Not enough to worry about. But enough. He looked at Sheridan and Sheridan held up a hand in the 'halt' sign.

'I'll take a look,' he said. 'You just set and take it easy.'

Angel sat back against the edge of the desk, while Sheridan took a hitch at his belt with his left hand, picked up the Greener, and went out into the bright sunlight, muttering something about popinjays. The Marshal walked out to the middle of the dusty street where Texas met Front and checked all three directions. Up towards the livery stable, Howie Cade was standing in front of two riders who were handing down their gunbelts to him. Howie walked over and hitched them over the rail outside the stable, then waved the riders on. Sheridan moved back towards the jail, leaning against the hitchrail and watching the two men come towards him. They had the dust of long travel on their clothes. Then he saw one of them was Danny Johnston: he didn't know the scrawny one with the bobbing Adam's apple.

'Johnston,' he said. 'You back again?'

'Come to parley, Marshal,' Johnston said.

'Talk away,' Sheridan said. He put the Greener down, stock first on the ground with the barrel resting against his leg, fishing in his pocket for a cigarette. When he looked up Danny Johnston had a sixgun in his hand and so did his companion. Both held them low, on the side of the high saddle pommels. No one in the street would even see them. They looked like two men passing the time of day with the Marshal. Danny Johnston smiled.

'No, Sheridan,' he said. 'Howie didn't turn his coat. That ain't him.'

The man dressed in Howie Cade's clothes was coming down the street, walking easily and without haste in the center of Front, hands never far from the matched sixguns. Sheridan looked at him and then at Johnston. His good left hand inched towards the barrels of the Greener and Johnston showed his teeth.

'You'd never make it, Sheridan,' he said.

Sheridan's eyes were bleak. But he didn't try for the shotgun. Inside the jail, Angel moved idly across to the window. He'd heard the voices outside. They were ordinary; the sound of desultory conversation. He glanced out of the window at the Marshal, facing the two horsemen whose faces were concealed from his line of sight by the *ramada* roof around the jail. But the tableau was wrong, and the figure of Howie Cade walking down the middle of the street was wrong. Sheridan was tensed, his left hand stiff and close to the shotgun at his left side, his shoulder down as though he had frozen in a movement. Then one of the horses shifted slightly, rearranging its feet, and he caught the wink of metal from one of the low-held sixguns.

'Where's Howie?' he heard Sheridan ask, and he could hear the control Sheridan was having to exercise on his voice to keep the sheer anger out of it.

'In a safe place,' one of the riders said.

'What do you want?' Sheridan said.

'You go lay that shotgun against the wall, Daniel,' the hidden rider said. 'Nice and easy. Then step out here into the street.'

Sheridan shrugged; there was nothing he could do but obey.

'Easy does it, Marshal,' one of the riders said. He backed his horse up slightly and Angel saw that it was Danny Johnston. That was all he needed to know. He moved on feet as silent as an Indian's towards the door, and eeled into the corridor. Burt Hugess watched him with wide eyes.

'What the hell . . . ?' he began, but he was addressing the air. Angel was already out of the door and on the dark-shadowed eastern side of the squat building. He moved easily to the corner. He could hear Danny Johnston speaking.

'—gets here, you and me will go into the jail nice and quiet and let Burt out. You do that, and maybe you'll live through this. Try anything else, and you won't. *Sabe?*'

Angel got down flat on the ground and eased an eye around the corner of the building: a man who looks around the edge of a building at his own height will attract the attention of another by being caught in the other's peripheral vision. Nobody ever expects anyone to peek around corners at ground level. He got their positions fixed in his mind. The man in Howie Cade's clothes was just coming past the Oriental and Angel knew it had to be now. His fingers fastened on the tattered horse blanket he'd snatched up as he came out into the corral. He pulled in his breath, long and deep, and then he stepped out into the open already moving fast, the blanket flapping as he whirled it around his head and whooped like a drunken Arapaho.

His sudden appearance, the startling sight of the flapping blanket and the unearthly noise had a predictable effect on the horses of the Flying H riders. Both of them went up into the air stiff-legged, ready to take off at a full gallop when they hit the ground. Neither Danny Johnston nor his sidekick had a cat's chance in hell of letting off a shot at Dan Sheridan, which was exactly what Angel had gambled on. Their instinctive reaction was to grab for the saddle horn and as they did so, he swept his gun from the holster, going down on one knee in a sweet, trained movement, clasping the wrist of his right hand in his left and cocking the gun in the same moment that the barrel lined up. His first shot blasted the skinny man sideways out of the leather with the astonishment of the moment still on his face. Johnston had perhaps a second longer to act and he did well enough, whacking a shot at Sheridan which took a piece of wood about six inches long and two inches wide out of one of the uprights of the *ramada* roof not more than a foot from Sheridan, who was already moving for the Greener. Before Danny Johnston could cock a gun in his hand again, Angel's second bullet tore through the muscles of Johnston's upper arm, smashed its way through the bones and ranged at a tangent upwards exiting in a bloody spraying mist just below his right ear. The Flying H man went off the horse as if someone had roped him, while the panicked horses stampeded off away towards the bridge over Cat Creek. Johnston humped up once in the dirt of Texas Street and then subsided even as Angel cocked his sixgun yet again. The man in Howie Cade's clothes had watched this awful scene in a frozen disbelief that melted suddenly as he realised he was standing in the centre of the plaza, and that Dan Sheridan had the Greener in his hand and was turning. He ran.

'Stop!' Sheridan yelled at the top of his voice. Johnny Evans heard the shout, but its meaning did not penetrate his panic-stricken mind for a long moment. Then as fast as he had turned to run he turned again with both of Howie Cade's sixguns in his hands and an animal snarl on his face that was torn away in a welter of mangled ribbons as Dan Sheridan laid the barrel of the Greener across his right forearm and pulled both of its triggers, almost blowing Johnny Evans into two separate pieces. Johnny went down flat on his back like one of those little metal figures in a fairground shooting booth and then it was over.

Sheridan stood there in the middle of the street with the smoking shotgun laid across his forearm, trying to figure out how it had all happened. He tossed the gun aside and started up the street and Angel watched him go. He saw people coming out of the houses and the saloons. Sherry Hardin came out on to the street and ran towards Sheridan. She told him something, and he turned away, going up an alley between the saloon and the next building. Sherry ran down towards Angel. In the curiously detached aftermath of the sudden action, he could see her face and body very clearly. She was a good runner, he noted. He watched the sweet soft movement of her breasts. She stopped beside him.

'Frank,' she said. She wasn't hysterical, upset, frightened.

Just glad to be with him. 'I saw it. Saw what happened.' She looked down at the torn, bleeding bodies of the three men. 'It was – so quick. They died so fast.'

He nodded. They always did, but there was no point in saying that to her. It was when you saw what the guns could do that you hated them. You hated the fact that you had to use them knowing what they could do. But you knew you had to do it.

'Where did Sheridan go?' he asked.

'It's all right,' she said. 'He's safe. He went after Howie.'

'Where is he?'

'They dragged him up the alley, I think. The Chinaman saw them. He came and told me. But it was too late for me to tell you. It all happened so fast.'

She shuddered a little, holding her own upper arms with her hands folded across her chest. There was no breeze and it was hot in the late afternoon sun.

'You need a drink,' he told her.

'Not as bad as Howie,' she said, and managed a smile.

'You're quite a girl, Sherry,' he said.

'You're quite a girl yourself, Angel,' she replied. This time the smile took, and it warmed her eyes. 'Maybe I'll buy *you* a drink.'

'Let's see if Howie's okay first,' Angel said.

She unfolded her arms and put them akimbo on her hips, pretending vexation.

'Don't you ever relax?' she asked him.

'Work first,' he said. 'Fun later.'

Up the street, Dan Sheridan was bringing Howie Cade towards the jail. He looked used up, and there was blood on his face and neck. But he was on his own two feet. He'd be okay, Angel judged.

'Well,' Sherry Hardin said when they came level. 'You sure are hell on clothes, Howie Cade.'

With three men dead in the street it didn't really seem appropriate to laugh. But the laughter bubbled up in them:

first Howie, weakly, and then Sheridan, Angel, all of them. They stood there in the street and slapped each other on the back, laughing at Sherry Hardin's mild little joke. Maybe it was relief. Maybe it was the reaffirmation of just being alive to laugh at all. Whatever it was, they laughed until tears ran down their cheeks. Mrs. Mahoney said it was almost indecent, so it was.

ELEVEN

USELESS, Howie Cade thought.

He sat in the jail alone, Sheridan and Angel were making a patrol of the town, the next to last one: what Sheridan called his 'sunset stroll'. Howie's hands were shaking. Useless, he thought, recalling how Danny Johnston's boys had taken him like a baby. He hadn't even been able to put up a fight. Fancy duds, buscadero belt and all, he was about as much use to Sheridan as a spavined mule. If it hadn't been for Angel, he and Sheridan would already be dead. They would have taken Dan as neat as a haircut, and it would have been his, Howie's, fault. The thought was like wormwood in his soul. He thought of a glass of whiskey and then he put the thought out of his mind, but it was still there somewhere in the background. He thought of Angel covering Dan Sheridan on the street. That was his job, Howie's job, not Angel's. Sheridan obviously figured Angel was more reliable. He probably was. He didn't have anything against Angel: he was good. It was a damned good job he'd shown up. Dan Sheridan wouldn't have lasted one day, let alone three, if the only backup he'd had was Howie Cade.

Goddamned useless, he thought.

'I used to be good,' he told himself. 'Damned good.'

He stood up and strapped on his gunbelt. Standing in a tight, poised crouch he drew the right hand gun. Good enough, he thought. As good as anyone needed to be. Yet they'd taken him like a snot-nosed kid, because he was slow, stupid, dumb. Useless.

The mental picture of the whiskey popped into the front of his brain again and he gave an order in his brain and it went away. He sat and stared at the calendar on the wall. Three days: Tuesday, Wednesday, Thursday, today, all but gone. Tomorrow was Friday. If they got through Friday, it would all be over. The train from El Paso to Kansass City, Missouri would chug into the depot at 11-45 on Saturday morning and once they had Burt Hugess on that train not even Larry Hugess was going to be able to do anything to stop them.

One more day, he thought.

Then he thought of a drink.

It wouldn't make any difference, he told himself. They wouldn't even miss me. If Dan told the truth, he'd admit that he can handle it just fine with Angel backing him up. It was Howie who couldn't cut it. They were carrying him, and they were avoiding telling him, that was all. Howie hoped he never had to stand there while Sheridan told him. One drink wouldn't hurt me, he thought. Might even help with these shaking hands.

They were taking their goddamned time with the patrol, too. Leave a man sitting alone in the jail, no telling who might kick the door in. Suppose Larry Hugess decided to put every man he had into the saddle and just ride in and take Madison apart stick by stick. Who the hell could stop him? How long could they hold out in the jail? Until they ran out of water, food, or ammunition. And what would Hugess do to them when they did? Anyway, who'd ever know if he took just one quick drink? Pretend he was just checking out one of the dives down below the depot, take a quick snort, move on.

One more day, he thought.

The town was quiet. He could hear the Professor banging away at something up-tempo in the Palace. He imagined the smoky warmth of the place, the yellow light of the oil lamps, the *crickety-crickety* sound of the chuckaluck box, the smell of sweat and sawdust and the smoky, hot taste of whiskey. No, he thought. But who the hell would care if I said yes?

He sat there and glowered at the wall until Sheridan and Angel came back. Sheridan used the interrupted knock that they had devised as a signal that it was safe to open up. Howie saw that it was dark outside now: the bright lights of the saloon across the way beckoned invitingly and he heard one of the girls laughing.

'Everything okay?' Sheridan asked, laying the Greener he'd been carrying down on the desk.

'Sure,' Howie said. His voice was surly. He didn't care if it was, he didn't care if Sheridan raised his eyebrows in surprise. The hell with Sheridan, if he felt like that.

'Any coffee?' Angel asked him.

'Go take a look,' Howie snapped. 'I ain't the maid.'

Angel held up both hands with the palms out.

'Okay, okay,' he said. 'Excuse me for living.'

He went across and poured some coffee into a tin mug. He raised an eyebrow at Sheridan, who nodded, yes, he'd take a cup. As their eyes met, Angel put the question on his face: *what's wrong with Howie*? Sheridan gave him an exaggerated shrug and a look of puzzlement as his answer so Angel shrugged and sat down, sipping at the steaming brew.

'Listen,' Howie said. 'I need some air.'

Sheridan looked at him.

'Wait on,' he said. 'I'll come with you.'

'No!' Howie said sharply. 'I'll just walk across the street to the Palace. Then back. Ain't nothing going to happen to me while I do that.'

He was conscious of the way Sheridan was watching him. He jerked his head, so Sheridan couldn't see what was in his eyes, but Sheridan had guessed.

'Howie,' he said. 'You want a drink, you go ahead and take one.'

'Who the hell said anything about . . .?' Howie Cade's outburst petered out. He looked at Sheridan and then he looked at Frank Angel. 'Oh, dammit all to Hell,' he said, and went out, slamming the heavy door behind him. Sheridan crossed the room to go after the deputy, and then, as if vexed with himself, stopped. He looked at his right hand and flexed it, steeling his expression against showing the pain.

'How does it feel?' Angel asked.

'Lousy,' Sheridan said. 'Just plain lousy.'

'Let him do it, Dan,' Angel said. 'Maybe he feels he has to.'

'Has to?' Sheridan ground out. 'You know what'll happen if he takes a drink, don't you? He'll take another and then another and then another, and that will be the end of him.'

'Maybe,' Angel said. 'I'm not so sure, though. I was watching his face. He can't bring himself to be jealous of me, which would solve his problem. But he's feeling as if somehow he's let you down. Maybe he reckons we don't need him. All that drives him towards the liquor. You don't drink the way Howie was drinking and then just quit. It hurts. It hurts for a long, long time.'

'You some kind of head-doctor, Angel?' Sheridan said, trying for a grin he had trouble pinning on.

'That's me,' Angel smiled. 'America's answer to Florence Nightingale.'

'Florence who?'

'Never mind,' Angel said. 'Give him ten, fifteen minutes. Then I'll walk over there and see how he's doing.'

Sheridan shrugged again. If Howie was really going to dive back into the bottle, it wouldn't take him any fifteen minutes. But he didn't tell Angel that. Angel would find out soon enough.

'Sabslu'lydiotichh,' Howie said.

'Sure is,' Angel replied. 'Easy, now.'

'Olihaddaglash,' Howie said. His eyes were unfocused, but he was trying very hard to get it across to Angel that he had only drunk one drink, and that he felt idiotic because it had knocked him sideways. He was draped around Angel like a wet towel, and Angel held him the best way he could as they went up the street to the Hotel. Howie's legs kept on snaking off to right or left, and he was no lightweight. By the time they made it to the door of the Hotel, Angel was sweating hard.

The little Chinaman opened the door and ran like a deer when Angel hefted Howie into a chair and said 'Coffee, and lots of it!' Sherry Hardin came down the stairs. She looked at Howie, who was sitting in the chair with his head back, eyes wide, mouth open, staring unseeingly at the ceiling.

'Oh, no,' she said.

'Oh, yes,' Angel said.

'I'll get—'

'I already told him,' Angel interrupted her. 'Coffee's on the way.'

'Why?' she wanted to know. 'Why, why?'

'Feelings of inadequacy, maybe,' he guessed. 'Just being down. I don't know. But don't worry. He hasn't had much. And the head this will give him will be all the discouragement he's going to need to stay away from the booze.'

'You hope,' she said.

'I hope,' he smiled. 'Till Saturday morning, anyway. After that he can go swim in the stuff as far as I'm concerned.'

A frown touched her forehead at his words.

'You'll leave?' she asked. 'On Saturday?'

'If all this is settled,' he said. 'Yes.'

'Ah,' Sherry Hardin said. 'That's not a lot of time to give a girl, Angel.'

'No,' he said. 'But it's all the time I've got.'

'I see,' she said softly. Then, as if shaking away thoughts she would rather not be thinking, she bustled across the room towards the little Chinaman, who was just coming in from the kitchen with a coffee-pot and two mugs on a wooden tray.

'All right, Chen,' she said. 'I'll do this. You make some more.'

As always, the little Chinaman went out without a word, his flat-soled shoes slip-slapping on the wooden floor. Sherry

Hardin stood with the tray in her hands and looked at Frank Angel. She had her head back, the way a woman will sometimes hold herself so the tears won't spill over her eyelids.

'Why don't you get on with whatever it is you've got to do, Frank,' she said, quietly. 'Before I start in bawling.'

He made as if to start towards her, but she gave a slight emphatic shake of her head. The copper hair caught glints of light from the hanging lamp. Angel made one of those 'okay, then' gestures with his head.

'I'll see you,' he said, and went out of there without looking back, eyes adjusting to the blackness outside, checking the street automatically. All clear. He stepped down off the porch and turned towards the jail. He could hear the Professor playing something slow. *Lorena,* was it?

The lancing flame of the sixgun was clearly visible in the alley across the street. The slug went past his head like an angry wasp and he saw the man, a dark running shape against the lighted windows of the Oriental. Almost without having to think about it, Angel had dropped to one knee and the sixgun was up and steadied, and he fired quickly. The man swerved, and Angel thought perhaps he might have nicked him.

'Hold it!' he yelled. The man hesitated and then ran into the Oriental. Angel legged it across the street as fast as he could go, and then went in underneath the batwings, flat on his belly with the gun up. There were six or seven people bayed against the wall. Not a gun in sight. He got up slowly, keeping the gun cocked. Three of them he knew by sight: townspeople. Their eyes were rolling in panic. They wanted out of there. Two of the others wore the standard range garb. They could have been Hugess riders. They could have been any damned thing at all. There were two others standing together near the door. One of them had a puffy face, his eyes blackened by bruises and a huge bloody scab across the bridge of his nose. Angel remembered him: he was the Hugess rider Howie had backhanded with the sixgun in the

Palace the night Nathan Ridlow had been killed. Dan Sheridan had pointed him out in the street.

'Where is he?' Angel said.

'Listen, mister—' Broken-Face began. 'We never—'

'Talk!' Angel said. 'Fast!'

'He went out the back door,' the man standing beside Broken-Face said, his voice pitched breathless.

'Show me,' Angel said, gesturing with the sixgun. One of the townspeople looked at Angel with a strange, throttled look, as if he wanted to say something but didn't know how. The man didn't speak. He looked down at the floor as if he was ashamed of himself.

'Over here,' Broken-Face said. He led the way around the bar and into a sort of hallway at the far side of which was a wooden door with two glass panels. The panels were of frosted glass, coloured green.

'Where does that lead?' Angel said.

'Out by the corral in back of the store,' Broken-Face said.

'And the man who ran into the saloon went out this way.'

'That's right,' the second man said, anxiously. 'Right through that door.'

'Alone, was he?'

'Why, sure he was,' Broken-Face said. 'I'd say you put a slug in his hide someplace, too. He was bleedin' pretty bad. Harvey seen it.'

'Better move along, Mister Angel,' Harvey added. 'He'll get clean away.'

'Sure,' Angel said. 'Lead the way.'

'What?' Harvey said.

'You heard me,' Angel told him. 'Open the door and walk on out there.'

'Who, me?' Harvey quavered. 'Listen, Mister Angel, I ain't got—'

Angel cocked the sixgun and in a savage gesture he jammed the barrel of the weapon into the overhanging gut of the big man.

'Uccchh,' Harvey said.

'Move!' Angel told him. 'You too, Beautiful!'

'Listen—' Broken-Face stammered.

'Why, the way you boys are acting, you'd think there was someone out there,' Angel said. 'You wouldn't have been trying to get me to walk into a deadfall, would you?'

'Hell, Angel!' Harvey said. 'We're tryin' to help you.'

'Sure,' Angel said. Without the slightest change of expression he shot Harvey in the backside. The scorching burn of the slug seared a yelping screech from the man, who fell backwards against the wooden wall, smearing it with blood. Broken-Face looked at his comrade aghast.

'Out!' Angel said.

'No,' Broken-Face said, holding up a hand with the palm towards Angel. 'Don't make us.'

'Out!' Angel said. His face was like something carved from granite. He eared back the hammer of the gun and Broken-Face cringed back. Harvey screamed in terror like a horse going over a cliff, a dark stain spreading downwards across the leg of his pants. He scrabbled for the door and yanked it open, shouting 'Don't shoot, boys, it's—!!' but that was as far as he got. As he yanked open the door and Angel stepped quickly back around the right angle of the wall, the stuttering boom of two or perhaps three shotguns tore the night apart. The flash from the guns illuminated the alley like summer lightning and the whickering hail of heavy slugs ripped Harvey and Broken-Face to ribbons, smashing their torn bodies against the bullet-riddled door like tattered puppets, filling the air with whispering lead and splintered wood and glass and the ugly sweet smell of fresh blood. Angel whirled as he heard footsteps pounding through the opening behind him, and Dan Sheridan skidded to a stop, the heavy Greener ready in his left hand. He looked at the carnage and his face set.

'Good Christ in Heaven!' he breathed. 'Who's – who was that?'

Angel told him. He told him what had happened.

'No use going after them,' he said. 'We know who they were.'

A thought occurred to him and he asked Sheridan a question.

'Sherry Hardin,' Sheridan said. 'She came lickety-split the minute she heard shooting. Howie's there with her, don't worry. Anyone tries to get near Burt's liable to get himself blown every damned way but up. Sherry's as nervous as a scalded cat, and Howie's just about the most miserable thing you ever saw.'

Angel nodded, moving out into the saloon. The two men he'd noted earlier were gone. The man who'd tried to speak to him came over.

'I tried,' he said, falteringly. 'But they had guns pointed at us, under the table. I'm sorry.' He was abject, standing there.

'Don't be,' Angel told him. 'You told me with your face. I guessed what was happening. The whole thing smelled of a set-up right from the start. If Hugess or his men wanted to shoot me in the street I reckon they could make a better job of it than that fellow did.'

'It's terrible,' the man said. 'Terrible. Can't something be done?'

'We're doing what we can,' Sheridan said. 'Everything we can.'

'We're afraid to walk the streets,' another man said.

'It's about time Larry Hugess was told he can't take the law into his own hands,' said the third.

'Well,' Sheridan said, no humour in his eyes. 'If you see him, you tell him that.'

He led the way back across to the jail, and Sherry Hardin opened the barred door. Her eyes were full of anxiety, but they softened when she saw the tall figure behind the Marshal. Sheridan saw the look and his own expression changed slightly. He'd been so damned wrapped up in what had been going on in Madison, that he'd missed the most important development of all. He realised he was going to have to do some adjusting of his thinking about Sherry Hardin. You could have cooked a meal on the warmth in her eyes as she looked at Angel.

'Listen,' he said, clearing his throat. 'Listen,' he said again, 'Howie here isn't going to sleep worth a damn tonight and neither am I. Why don't you grab a decent night's sleep, Angel? I can manage things here. You can probably. . . .' He tailed off with a wry grin as he realised he was selling it too hard. Angel was looking at him with surprise, and he grinned at Sheridan's guilty expression.

'Matchmaking, Dan?' Angel said. 'Isn't that sort of out of your line of country?'

'Go to hell,' Sheridan said.

'Angels don't go to hell, Dan,' came the reply. 'Only town Marshals who read romantic novels.'

'Hey,' came the injured voice of Howie Cade. 'Isn't anybody going to talk to me?'

'Sure, Howie,' Sheridan said, waving Angel and Sherry Hardin out of the jail. 'Sure.' He gave them a so-long signal and as he closed the door and barred it again, they heard him say, 'I'm going to talk to you, all right. And you'd better believe it!'

They walked back to the Hotel together. Once in a while their hands brushed together, or their shoulders kissed. They didn't speak the whole way. The town was silent now. The Professor had quit playing at the Palace. The lights were all out in the Oriental. They went inside together.

'Well,' Angel said.

Before he could say anything else, or Sherry reply, the little Chinaman came out from his kitchen. His button eyes were shining and he looked at Angel with unconcealed admiration.

'You want eat?' he said. 'I fix.'

It was the first time Angel had ever heard him speak. He said so.

'Ah,' said Chen. 'Special 'casion.'

'Well, thanks, Chen. But I'm not hungry. I could use a drink, though.'

'You bet!' Chen said. He scurried over to a cupboard and clinked about with bottle and glasses. He brought a drink for Sherry too.

'Chen,' she said warningly. 'What is all this?'

'Celebrate living,' he said. 'Sleep good.'

He managed somehow to include Angel and the girl in the one phrase and smiled as he shuffled off back to his kitchen, leaving them looking at each other. They finished the drinks and put the glasses down on one of the tables.

'Good night, Sherry,' Angel said.

'You're tired,' she said. It wasn't a question. His eyes were dark with fatigue. The tensions of the day, the sharp angry moments of action had all to be paid for. He nodded in reply.

'I could use some sleep,' he said.

She turned away, picking up the glasses, speaking with her back to him.

'My door's right opposite yours,' she said. 'I'll leave it open.'

She didn't look at him as she brushed past and hurried up the stairs. He waited until he heard her door open and close and then went up. Outside her door, he paused. He could hear her moving on the bed and he touched the doorknob, turning it. She hadn't been lying: it wasn't locked.

He turned away and went into his own room. It looked sparse and cold. The curtains lifted slightly in the faint night breeze and he could hear the far-off yowl of a hunting bob-cat. He pulled off his boots, thinking about Larry Hugess, wondering what the big man was planning, how he would have reacted to the death of so many of his men, the failure of each of his attemptes to kill Sheridan, or Howie, or himself.

Maybe Hugess had decided to give up, now. Maybe he would let them put Burt on the train and take him to the Capital for trial. And maybe the moon was made of green cheese, Angel grinned tiredly. He lay on his bed and watched the square of the moonlit wall, his thoughts jumbled. He kept trying to concentrate on tomorrow, to put himself into Larry Hugess' place and anticipate the man's plans, thoughts, ideas. But all the time the face of Sherry Hardin floated into his mind and he saw her toss her head and her hair catching the sunlight.

He must have dozed because a slight sound woke him.

He was awake instantly, the gun in his hand. But the noise had not been in the room. Outside. He eased off the bed without making a creak, moving across the room close to the wall where no floorboard would protest his weight. Easy, easy, easy, he thought, as he turned the doorknob easy and silently. There was no one outside. The place was as silent as an undisturbed tomb. Sherry Hardin's door was ajar. He could see the counterpane turned back. The bed was empty. Frowning, he eased along the hall and down the stairs, keeping to the wall side of each tread. The foot of the staircase was a pool of utter blackness but his sense told him there was someone in it. He could hear the faint sound of breathing; his keen hearing told him it was not the rasping tensed breath of a hiding man.

At the foot of the stairs, swaddled up in a huge red-and-black blanket that looked as if it belonged on a Christmas sleigh, was Sherry Hardin. She was fast asleep, and her long copper hair spilled across the checkered material like a cascade of dark golden water. She had a nickel-plated Colt's Peacemaker with a nine-inch barrel in her hand. It lay in her lap as big as a cannon, and Angel smiled in the darkness at her brave folly.

'Sherry,' he said softly.

She stirred in her sleep and he took the heavy gun out of her nerveless hand. Warmth glowed from her curled-up body as he lifted her, and she said his name as she burrowed her face into the angle of his neck. Her lips were dry but he felt her kiss him as he started up the stairs. Although she was not a small girl, it seemed to him that she weighed hardly anything at all.

TWELVE

ONE more day, Larry Hugess told himself.

He sat in the big, sprawling living room of his ranch, face set in a heavy scowl, and faced the unalterable fact that he had to admit that a crippled Marshal, a reformed drunk, and a Government snooper had not only faced, but overcome the very best men he could put up against them. But Larry Hugess was not a stupid man. Bull-headed, obstinate, full of pride, he was all of those and knew it. But not stupid. He realised now that he had been using a sledgehammer to kill an ant, and it had cost him dear: very dear. If he did not now use his brain instead of his strength it would cost him the rest of what he owned and he was not about to let that happen. He slouched in the heavy chair, legs stretched out in front of him, a hunting dog asleep with its head on his burnished leather boots, a big man rendered powerless by insignificant enemies, as powerless as is the dog to make war on the flea.

They had brought him the news of his setbacks, of the death of good men hesitantly, perhaps instinctively knowing the fate of bearers of bad tidings. Larry Hugess had heard them out impassively. The death of such as Johns, Evans, even Johnston moved him more than the death of one of his steers. They took the money: there fore they knew the risk. Losing them was a setback, but nothing vital. There were plenty of men willing to sell their guns to a man who paid well. If only he had more time!

He reflected again upon the unassailable fact that time was running out. The train would arrive and unless Burt was freed by then, he was through. Not even Larry Hugess could take on the Atchison Topeka & Santa Fe Railroad. He had considered, and rejected, the idea of mounting all his men, taking over the town, and daring Sheridan to walk down the street to the depot with his prisoner. Sheridan, with Angel alongside him, would do just that, forcing Larry Hugess to kill him out in the open where the whole town could see it done. Angel, too would have to be killed, and Larry Hugess wanted no witness who could inform the Department of Justice of the circumstances of the Government man's death. Life was too short and too precious to spend every hour of it looking over one's shoulder for another pursuer from the Justice Department. Yet the equation remained, no matter how he approached it, no matter how he turned it over in his mind. The cement holding together the barrier to realising his intent was Frank Angel. Remove Angel from the equation and it collapsed: Sheridan was a good man, but he couldn't fight one-handed. Cade wasn't even worth wasting time thinking about. So it came ineluctably back each time to the same solution: Angel must die. If Angel did not die, then Larry Hugess had no future, and he could not, would not face that possibility. He had worked too hard for the things he had.

He looked around the room in which he sat, as if seeing it for the first time. It was a fine, high room, painted white and styled in the Spanish fashion, with arched doorways and black fretted ironwork at the windows. A massive oil painting of himself hung above the fireplace and dominated the room: Larry Hugess with imperious stance and haughty eyes, dressed in the long white coat and low-crowned hat of a Mississippi plantation-owner, head thrown back, hand on holstered hip, looking out across some spacious vista, confident, unassailable, strong. The fireplace itself was big enough to roast half a steer, although it had been many years since the blackened cooking pots had been used, the carefully-arranged logs set afire. A fine imported carpet covered the red-tiled floor, and the furniture was good, hand-hewed oak that set solid and dependable around the room. The table was huge, like one you might see in a refectory; it had seated twenty many times, for when Larry Hugess entertained he did so royally and without stint. One wall of the room was filled with shelves of books in fine tooled-leather bindings. Huge oil lamps hung from the beamed ceiling. At night, they picked glinting highlights from good silver and fine crystal. By day, the big windows let in the burning sunlight to fill the room with molten gold. Larry Hugess loved this room, this house. He had worked all his life to own what it contained and what it represented. He had sweated and he had lied, he had worked and he had cheated, fixed what needed fixing and paid whatever prices had to be paid and he had come to where he was now because he was strong and ruthless, lavishly generous when necessary, his table rich, his wines impeccably selected, his guest-book filled with all the right names. Before very much longer this Territory was going to send someone to the Congress of the United States and when it did, that man was going to be Larry Hugess. It would be the fruition, the realisation of everything he had worked for, the reward for all the years of doing favours, of wheeling, dealing, fixing – yes, and even killing, he thought – that had passed since he had planted his marker on this land and begun to build the Flying H with little more behind him but a milch cow and a bellyful of guts. He had put his life, his wealth, his sweat, his blood into this thing and he would have his reward. But not if Angel lived.

One more day.

He admitted to just the faintest sense of unease. He took great care to conceal any sign of it, but it was there just the same. He dare not show weakness in front of such men as rode for him these days: they were rats with an extrasensory perception for weakness, who would run from a sinking ship as cold-bloodedly as they knew he would abandon them if he had to. He got up and paced the floor, lighting a thick Havana cigar from a humidor on a Florentine table beside his chair. The dog rolled back and looked at him, realised he wasn't going out, and went back to sleep.

'Good boy,' Hugess said, automatically.

He looked at the whiskey decanter and then shook his head, angry at himself. There weren't any solutions to the problem in there. Afterwards, he told himself, afterwards he would get monumentally, roaring drunk in celebration. But not now: time was short and he had to come up with some way of defusing Frank Angel. There was something: something one of the men had told him. He had laid it aside, the way a man will lay aside a useful tool in case he cannot do what he wants to do with his hands.

He went over the surly, monosyllabic reports from his riders, trying to remember what they had said, word for word, when they had brought him the news that Angel had eluded the trap at the Oriental and caused the death of two more men.

Ken Finstatt had stood in the middle of the room, beneath the portrait of his master, turning his Stetson around in his hands, putting into mumbling words this latest catastrophe. Hugess had heard him through in silence: the Justice Department man coming out of the Hardin place, the decoy shot and Angel's unexpectedly accurate return shot that had clipped Stu Fennick's arm badly enough to put him out of any further action. He heard how Harvey Macrae and Gene Sanchez had been stampeded out into the alley by Angel and cut down by the blasting shotguns of Ken Finstatt and his sidekicks.

'We skedaddled out of that alley,' Finstatt had told him. 'Round to the jail, ready to make our play with Angel dead. You can imagine how we was dumbstruck when he came out of the Oriental large as life an' twice as ugly.'

'And then?' Hugess had asked.

'Well,' Finstatt told him. 'Nothin' much. Angel went on back up to the ho-tel. Sheridan an' Cade was back in the jail. We was stuck.'

Hugess nodded. They never took any initiative, men like

Finstatt. You told them what they had to do and they tried to do it. If it worked, they came back like children with a puzzle solved. If it did not, they came back so you could tell them what to do next.

'Of course,' Hugess had said, silkily sardonic, 'it never occurred to you to finish Angel off in the street, did it?'

'Sure it did!' Finstatt protested. 'Exceptin' your orders was that if we got Angel, it didn't have to look too . . . too . . .'

'Blantant was the word I used,' Hugess said. 'Although how you could be less blatant than to lie in ambush with three shotguns I fail to see.'

'Yea,' Finstatt said, either missing the sarcasm or avoiding it. 'Well. If we'd've gone for Angel, we'd've had to kill that Hardin woman too.'

'Sherry Hardin?'

'Right! She was walkin' up the street to the ho-tel with Angel, right close, cosy as two cats in a basket.'

That was it!

Larry Hugess slapped his thigh and the hound looked up at him reproachfully. Hugess didn't even see it. He knew he had the lever for which he had been looking in his mind, knowing he had laid it aside there for possible use.

'And what is that supposed to mean?' he had asked Finstatt.

'Well,' Finstatt said, uneasily. He put the first bits of a leer on his face, as though needing permission to add the rest. Finstatt was aware that Larry Hugess knew and perhaps even had ideas about Sherry Hardin.

'Well?' Hugess had snapped, knowing why Finstatt hesitated and implicitly giving him permission to continue. He felt like a pimp for encouraging the man, sensing what Finstatt would imply. It was true: Sherry Hardin was a handsome woman, and he had often thought how well she would look at his side. An intelligent, beautiful woman could be a great advantage to a man setting out on a political career. He had set aside his intention to let her know of his interest for an appropriate time which had never come. But he was aware of her, and knew she had been aware of him.

'Well,' Finstatt said, letting the rest of the leer write itself around his mouth and eyes, 'I'd say the widder Hardin's got the hots for our Mister Angel!'

For a moment, he was afraid he'd gone too far: Hugess' eyes blazed with anger, but the big man quickly got control of his emotions.

'Guesswork, or fact?' he'd forced himself to say.

'Fact,' Finstatt said, openly smiling now. He'll nudge me in the ribs with his elbow next, Hugess thought, repelled.

There was another question, but Hugess couldn't bring himself to answer it. It didn't matter; what mattered was the fact that there was an emotional tie between Sherry Hardin and Frank Angel. How strong it was he would have to find out, gamble on. The more he thought about it, though, the likelier it all seemed. The Hardin girl had always been a stand-off, even Sheridan hadn't got really close to her and it wasn't too hard to figure he'd tried. She was pleasant to everyone – Hugess included – but never really unbent to anyone. Maybe Angel had touched the trigger that no other man had been able to find. It was more than possible and that was enough for Larry Hugess. Emotion drained out of him now and decision rushed to fill the vacuum. He gave a great shout of triumph that brought his Mexican housekeeper running into the room, wide-eyed with alarm.

'Oh, *Señor* Hugess!' she exclaimed. 'You frighten me bad!'

Larry Hugess was smiling with pleasure and anticipation and he slapped her on her ample rump.

'*Es nada,* Maria, *nada!*' he chortled. 'Bring me some coffee. Finstatt, get in here!'

This last he yelled out of the open window and Ken Finstatt, working in the corral across the wide open space in front of the house, looked up and shambled into a run.

'Somethin' wrong?' he said as he came into the house.

'Just the opposite,' Hugess said. 'Saddle my horse. Get the men ready. We're going into Madison!'

'Madison?' Finstatt said. 'What we goin' to do?'

'Do?' Larry Hugess roared. 'Do? We're going to fetch my brother home for dinner tonight, that's what we're going to do!'

Ken Finstatt looked at Larry Hugess for a long moment, the carefully-judged look of a man weighing another for any hint of bluff or braggadocio but not showing what he is searching for. There was no question of Larry Hugess' confidence – it radiated from him like heat from a fire.

'Well?' he growled. 'What the hell are you waiting for?'

'Nothin', boss,' Finstatt said. 'Not a damned thing!'

He hurried from the house to do Larry Hugess' bidding. Whatever it was Hugess aimed to do, it sure looked like he didn't expect it to backfire. Well, Finstatt thought as he yelled orders to the men in the bunkhouse, it sure as hell better not.

THIRTEEN

ONE more day, Frank Angel told himself.

They were sitting in the jail with nothing very much to do, taking their time about doing it. The sun was already well up towards noon, and the town was as quiet as a baby's bedroom. Howie Cade was in fact half-asleep. He'd kind of snuggled himself up in a blanket, propped his feet upon the desk, and tilted his hat forward over his eyes. Dozing, he called it. Once in a while the other two heard him make a noise like a fretful sigh.

Sheridan had fashioned himself a smoke. He was still clumsy but he could use his injured hand some now. He kept practising a draw, but he was nowhere near being ready to do it in earnest. He looked across at Frank Angel, but didn't speak. Angel's eyes were blank, looking inward. He wondered what Angel was thinking about.

Angel was thinking about Larry Hugess. About everything Sherry Hardin had told him, everything Sheridan had told him, everything old Nate Ridlow had told him, and they all added up to the same thing: a man who went after what he wanted and never gave up until he got it. With twenty-four hours between train time and now, Hugess had to move soon. He'd tried every damned way there was to cut one or two of them down, leaving the way clear to his brother in the cells. With failure jeering at him, Hugess would react. He might even over-react, Angel thought. He thought of Hugess mounting up all his riders and making a concerted attack on the jail. Thirty men, maybe, against three: but three with an ace-in-the-hole of great strength. Larry Hugess knew that if push came to shove, Burt Hugess wouldn't come out of the jail alive, either. He tried to put himself in the rancher's place. What other methods could he try?

Hold up the train? It seemed highly unlikely. A man with as much at stake as Hugess might risk everything in the town he controlled; but he wouldn't want to take on the kind of investigation that follows a train holdup. Delay the train? Possible, but to what purpose? In the end, he was still faced with the impasse: Burt in the jail and three men determined to keep him there in with him.

Hugess might string his men all the way along the street and across it up by the depot, dare them to try to take Burt on to the train. That wouldn't work, and he figured Hugess knew it as well. All Sheridan had to do was lash himself to Burt, cock the hammers on the Greener and jam the barrels under Burt's chin, then walk up the street to the depot. One try at stopping him and he could spread Burt Hugess over about half an acre of the Territory. Impasse again.

'You think Hugess would want to take us even if it meant killing Burt to do it?' he asked Sheridan. The Marshal's eyes widened at the unexpected question, and he pursed his lips while he considered it.

'I reckon not,' he said finally.

'No way,' Howie said from under his hat. 'Larry Hugess is a man too full o' pride to defeat hisself thataway.'

'What I figured,' Angel said, lapsing into silence again.

'I reckon he'll rush us,' Sheridan said, as if reading Angel's mind.

'How come?'

'Look at it from his point of view,' Sheridan said. 'Time's running out fast. He's got to commit: it's piss-or-git-off time. He's probably wondering just how genuine my promise was to shoot Burt if the going got too rough. Maybe he'll even look at it as a benefit: I shoot Burt, ain't no way he can be tried and disgrace the Hugess name.'

'Hard to swallow,' Howie said, without moving. 'But possible.'

'It's about all he's got left to shoot with,' Sheridan said.

'And the longer we got to wait, the likelier it is that that's what he'll do.'

If he agreed with them, Angel didn't say so. He had withdrawn again, and his eyes were hooded. What would Hugess do? Where would he make his play? When would it happen?

He didn't have to wait too long for an answer.

Larry Hugess and his men holed up in the big warehouse by the depot while Finstatt did what needed to be done. It was easy as slicing pie. They went around in back of the Hotel, where they could hear the cheerful clatter of the pots and pans as Chen went about getting the midday meals ready. Finstatt had two men with him: Lee Shepard and Jim Landy. Landy rapped on the screen door and Shepard and Finstatt flattened themselves against the wall on either side.

'What you want?' the Chinaman asked Landy.

'Can you spare me a minute?' Landy asked politely. 'Just a minute?'

'Hokay,' Chen said, cheerfully, and stepped out. His knees folded as Finstatt smacked him behind the ear with the barrel of his sixgun, and he fell into the arms of the waiting men. In two minutes Landy had him tied securely and they rolled him out of the way, going into the kitchen on careful feet, easing open the swing door that led into the dining room.

'Right,' Finstatt whispered.

The place was empty: Sherry Hardin was humming to herself as she moved around the tables, setting cutlery in place and puting salt and pepper cruets in the centre of the tablecloth. She turned without panic as she heard their footsteps, thinking it was the Chinaman.

'Chen,' she said, 'I think we—'

The words trailed into nothing as she saw the three men and they saw her chest rise as she drew in her breath.

'That would be very silly, lady,' Finstatt said, showing her the cocked sixgun.

'Wh – what do you want?' she said. Then, angrily, 'What have you done to Chen?'

'That the Chinee?' Landy grinned. 'He's takin' a nap.'

'If you've hurt him,' Sherry Hardin said fiercely, 'I'll—'

'Lady, don't try my patience,' Ken Finstatt said. 'Just quit jabberin' an' come with us.'

'Where? You're Hugess' men, aren't you? What's this all about?' she said.

'Just move your ass, lady,' Finstatt said. 'Beggin' your pardon. We ain't got all day, an' the boss wants to see you.'

Her chin came up. 'And if I refuse to go?'

Finstatt shook his head, as if bored with such folly.

'Then I'll bend this sixgun over your pretty little head, lady,' he told her. 'An' we'll carry you over there.'

'I'll walk,' she said quickly. 'Just don't any of you touch me.'

There was a revulsion in her voice and Finstatt caught the tone. He reacted sharply.

'Not with a bargepole, lady,' he snapped. 'We don't want none of that Government snooper's leavin's!'

He caught the hand she swung at his face and held it, effortlessly, as she cursed him. Then he shoved her away with an impatient gesture.

'All right,' he said. 'You've had your fun. Now walk!'

Sherry Hardin looked at him and then at the other two. They returned her burning contempt with complete indifference and she shrugged.

'Very well,' she said.

'That's better,' Ken Finstatt told her. 'It's only up the street.'

'Marshal!'

Sheridan let his rocked-back chair come four-square to

the ground and used its impetus to propel him forward on to his feet. The hammering on the door continued.

'Who's out there?' Sheridan called, keeping to one side of the door. Angel was already on his feet, and Howie was poised warily by the door that led to the cells, the Greener in his hands and every trace of sleepiness gone from his stance.

'It's Gardner, Marshal,' the voice came. 'Johnny Gardner!'

'Speak your piece,' Sheridan said.

'I brung you a message,' Gardner said through the wood. 'From Larry Hugess. You better open up, Marshal.'

Sheridan looked at Angel with raised eyebrows, and Angel nodded. He gave Howie Cade the signal and Howie propped his back against the wall, levelling the heavy sawn-off on the doorway which Sheridan was now about to open. If anyone was using Gardner to gain entrance to the jail, he wasn't going to make it more than about two paces inside. Angel, too, was ready with cocked sixgun, and Sheridan was behind the door with another. Gardner paled when he saw the arsenal staring at him.

'Hey,' he said weakly. 'Hold on there.'

He was alone, and Sheridan closed the door behind the saloonkeeper.

'Larry Hugess is in town?' Sheridan asked.

'That's right, Marshal,' Gardner nodded. 'An' he sent me to give you his message. His ultimatum.'

'Let's hear it,' Angel said.

'Hugess said to tell you he wants Burt delivered to him at the warehouse by two o'clock. Not a minute later. You all got to walk up there unarmed. Hugess will be waiting for you.'

'It's a good message,' Howie Cade said. 'If you believe in fairy tales.'

'Which Hugess doesn't,' Sheridan reminded him grimly. 'What's the rest of it, Johnny?'

'Said to tell you he's got Sherry Hardin up there,' Gardner

said. 'Said to tell you to do what he says or he's going to give her to his boys.'

'He *what*?' Sheridan grabbed Gardner's shirt and pulled the man towards him. 'He said *what*?'

'Listen, Marshal, this ain't none of my doin'!' Gardner screeched. 'They told me to bring you the message, that's all. I got nothing to do with it!'

Sheridan thrust the quaking saloonkeeper to one side. He looked at Frank Angel, who had not spoken. Angel's eyes were dark, burning with a deep fire somewhere a long way inside.

'Jesus, Dan,' Howie Cade said. 'What we goin' to do?'

'What time is it?' Sheridan asked, absently, his thoughts furiously busy.

'Twenty before two,' Johnny Gardner supplied, trying to be helpful, the gold hunter watch picking up a faint glint of sunlight from a crack in one of the shutters.

'Twenty minutes,' Sheridan muttered. 'That doesn't give us any damned time at all.'

They looked at each other in silence, and then Howie Cade broke it by addressing the saloonkeeper.

'Johnny,' he said, measureless contempt in his voice. 'You done what was expected of you. Now get out o' here!'

Gardner nodded, backing away towards the door.

'I'd help, you boys know that,' he chattered. 'I'd be glad to do anything I could, except I'm no fighting man, you know that, Sheridan, I never carry a gun, I—'

'Get out of here, Johnny,' Sheridan said, offhandedly. There didn't seem to be any threat in the Marshal's voice at all, but Gardner must have seen something in Sheridan's eyes because he gave a squeak of panic and scuttled out of the jail like a rabbit. They heard his feet stumble on the boardwalk outside the building and then the silence came down like a tangible thing. The room smelled of tension.

'Get him out,' Angel said, harshly.

'Listen,' Sheridan said.

'Get him out,' Angel repeated. 'Howie: do it!'

Howie Cade looked at Angel and then at Sheridan.

'Listen, Frank,' Sheridan said. 'He wouldn't. He wouldn't do it.'

Angel just looked at him; the deep fire was still seething behind his eyes. He looks as if he wants ti kill someone, Sheridan thought. With his bare hands.

'You a betting man?' Angel asked.

Sheridan thought about that for a moment. He knew what Angel was asking him: was he prepared to pay up if he lost the bet? He thought about Larry Hugess, and what Larry Hugess had done already to try to free his brother. He thought about all the other things Larry Hugess had done in a lifetime of being top man, getting what he wanted. And he knew he wasn't about to take that kind of chance with Sherry Hardin as the stake. This game was sudden death: and you don't back long shots in it.

'All right,' he said. 'Get him out here, Howie.'

Howie Cade nodded and lifted the ring of keys off the hook. The other two stood silently, looking at but not seeing each other as Howie opened the cell door and brought a grinning Burt Hugess into the office.

'Well,' Burt said, arms akimbo and a wide smile on his face. 'Well, well.' There was no way he couldn't have heard what Gardner had told them, no way he could have missed their evaluation of the situation. He was sure Larry had them cold and he was enjoying it hugely.

'Haw,' he exploded. The laughter, the sheer delight in their predicament, welled up in him. 'Haw, haw, haw!' Burt went. 'Haw, haw, *hucccccchhh!*'

He hadn't seen Angel move, hadn't even sensed the coiled tension in the man, but Angel's hand, the fingers held in a certain way, had jabbed out horizontally at heart level, moving no more than six inches but striking Burt Hugess' chest above the sternum with a force that momentarily stopped Burt's heart. He flailed backwards against the edge of Sheridan's desk, eyes popping with panic as his astonished body tried to obey the commands of the brain and get blood pumping from the shocked muscles of his heart. He went down on one knee, head hanging, labouring wheezes breaking from his throat. He sounded like a gutshot horse. Angel stood over the fallen man, his hand drawn back. He was centimetres away from delivering the second blow that would have snapped Burt Hugess' neck like a dried cornhusk when Dan Sheridan laid a very, very gentle hand on his forearm and spoke his name. Then again, watching carefully, poised, as the killing anger died in Angel's eyes and he came back from wherever he'd gone.

'All right,' Angel said. His shoulders slumped a fraction of an inch. 'All right.'

Burt Hugess was climbing to his feet, coughing, wheezing, water dribbling from his nose, his eyes wide and shocked.

'You bas . . .' he said. 'You fuckin—'

'—Burt!!' Sheridan snapped. He nodded to Howie, who grabbed Hugess' arms.

'Turn me loose!' Burt Hugess scrawed. 'Let me at that f—!'

'That's all,' Sheridan said, and showed Burt the bore of the sixgun. The triple click of the hammer going back stilled Burt's outburst. Then his sneer pasted itself back across his face.

'You won't use that, Sheridan,' he said. 'You don't dare use a gun on me.'

'Not to kill you,' Sheridan admitted judiciously. 'But I might just wound you some.' He said it with a cold grin that checked Burt Hugess for a moment. Then the bluster came back.

'Yeah,' Burt said. 'You got the whip hand now, Sheridan. For the moment. You and this . . . this pile of ordure.' He jerked his thumb at Angel, but from his appearance it was difficult to know whether Angel had even heard the words. 'Well just wait, that's all,' Burt Hugess ranted on. 'Just wait till we get up the street. Wait till I'm the one with the gun. I'll shoot your goddamned balls off, Sheridan. All of you.'

'That'll be the day,' Sheridan said, and tapped Hugess lightly alongside the ear with the barrel of the gun. It wasn't a hard enough blow to stun, but both of the other men in the room heard the audible *clack* as Burt Hugess' teeth jarred together from the impact. His eyes crossed slightly, unfocusing, and he reeled on his feet.

'Mind your manners, now,' Sheridan told him.

He turned towards Frank Angel. Angel was standing pretty much in the same position that he had been when Sheridan had stopped him from killing Hugess.

'Frank?' he said.

Angel looked up. There was nothing in his eyes at all. They were empty and cold, as if the man was gone to prepare some killing ground a long way away.

'Frank,' Sheridan said again. 'It's five before two. Time to move out.'

Howie Cade nodded and moved over to the door. He threw it wide, as if contemptuous of what might be outside. The sunlight flooded in, and Burt Hugess drew himself up, ready to walk out proud and tall. Sheridan laid his shotgun on one of the desks, unsheathed his handgun and laid it alongside the Greener. Howie Cade followed suit. Both men stood on the threshold of the jail and looked at Frank Angel. After what seemed like a very long time Angel lifted the sixgun from his holster and put it down on the desk. Then he looked at the Marshal.

'Let's go,' he said.

The four of them stepped out into the naked sunlight.

FOURTEEN

'HERE they come,' Ken Finstatt said.

He'd followed Larry Hugess' orders to the letter, and he had to admit that it was going sweet as wild honey. He had a man on each of the northern walls of the buildings between the jail and the depot on Front Street. As Burt Hugess and the three lawmen passed them, these men fell into step behind, guns trained on the backs of the group.

Frank Angel counted them as they stepped out of the shadows into the dusty sunlight: two, three, four, seven. He shook his head in a signal to Sheridan. Too many by far, he was saying. Sheridan gave an almost imperceptible nod: damned right, he was agreeing. By the time they passed the livery stable, there was no question that the three lawmen were the prisoners and Burt Hugess their captor. He strode ahead of them, head back, as if daring someone in one of the houses to make a face, shout an epithet. Nobody did. The street was as empty as if there had been a plague.

'Larry!' Burt Hugess shouted.

Larry Hugess stepped out on to the street. He opened his arms wide, like a proud parent does with a kid coming out of school. Burt Hugess threw his arms around his older brother, and they beamed into each other's face, pounding away at each other's shoulders as if they had been parted for years. Angel, Sheridan and Cade stood in the brassy sunlight under the guns of the Flying H men and watched the performance.

Then, finally, the brothers stepped apart.

'What do we do with these three, boss?' Ken Finstatt called.

Burt Hugess' face darkened.

'Give me a gun,' he hissed. 'Give me a gun, somebody!'

He glared at Frank Angel as he spoke.

'Don't be a fool, Burt!' his brother snapped. 'Stop that!'

Burt Hugess scowled, but he stood for it. Whatever else, he obeyed his older brother, Angel saw.

'Hugess,' he said. 'We handed over your brother. Now you hand over Miss Hardin.'

Larry Hugess turned, inspecting him thoroughly, walking around him the way a man buying a horse will walk around it, weighing up its good and bad points.

'So you're Angel,' he said, a soft sneer in his voice. 'You don't look so much.'

'What about Miss Hardin, Hugess?' Dan Sheridan said.

'She's all right, Marshal,' Hugess told him silkily. 'You don't really believe I planned to hurt her, do you?'

'I'd believe just about anything anybody told me about you,' Sheridan replied evenly, noting with satisfaction that his shaft had struck home. Larry Hugess' face darkened with anger, but he controlled it. He turned to Finstatt.

'Bring the girl out here,' he said. 'We'll escort her back to the Hotel.'

'Larry?' Burt Hugess said, disbelief in his voice. 'You going to turn these three loose?'

'Wait,' his brother said, non-committally. They stood in the street while Ken Finstatt went into the warehouse and came out with Sherry Hardin. She shook his hand off as he touched her, plain disgust written all across her face. Her copper hair was like fire in the sunshine. She saw the three men standing in the centre of the ring of armed guards and ran towards them. Larry Hugess nodded to one of his men: a rifle-barrel came up, barring her way. Sherry Hardin looked at Larry Hugess and said something very unladylike. If it bothered the rancher, he didn't show it.

'Sherry,' Frank Angel said. 'You all right? They didn't hurt you?'

'No,' she said. There was a faint puzzlement in her voice.

'Did they tell you they were going to?'

'Something like that,' Angel admitted.

'You should have told them to go to hell,' she blazed, and in spite of their predicament the three lawmen smiled.

'Maybe you're right at that,' Sheridan said.

'I'm sorry to interrupt this touching little scene,' Larry Hugess interposed smoothly. 'But we must see Miss Hardin back to the Hotel.'

'Why don't we come with you?' Howie Cade offered. 'Be no trouble.'

Larry Hugess regarded him bleakly.

'I'm glad to see liquor hasn't ruined your macabre sense of humor, Cade,' he said. 'I trust you'll still be seeing the funny side of things a few hours from now.'

He turned to Sherry Hardin, and with a slight bow, indicated that she should start to walk towards the Hotel. Sherry Hardin's head came up: defiance was written all over her face as she tossed her coppery hair.

'I'm not moving until you turn Frank – until you turn these men loose.'

'Ah, my dear girl,' Hugess said, urbanely. 'No, no. You see, until Burt and I leave town, the Marshal and his helpmates are our guarantee of safe passage. If I turn them loose, they will feel impelled to try and arrest my brother again. Perhaps myself also. Isn't that so, Marshal?'

'You bet your ass it's so!' Sheridan growled.

'You see, Miss Hardin,' Hugess said, spreading his hands as if apologising for Sheridan's rudeness. 'I'm powerless. So I merely wish to see that you get safely to your door. Then,' he turned towards his brother as he spoke, 'my brother and I are going home!'

'Tell her the rest, Hugess,' Angel said. The rancher whirled around at the sound of Angel's sardonic tone, anger building behind his eyes again.

'The rest of what?' he snapped.

'Tell her why you and your brother want to parade down

the centre of Front Street,' Angel rasped. 'Tell her you want to show this town once and for all who's the master. Tell her you're putting on a parade and she's only one of the clowns. I'm right, aren't I?'

Larry Hugess permitted himself a smile. A wintry smile, perhaps; but a smile for all that.

'Mister Angel,' he said, with a nod of acknowledgement. 'You're shrewd. And you're right, of course. I want Madison to see the Hugess brothers walking down the middle of its main street free. I want these people to see, to realise that the only Law here is my law. As they will. They will. And now, Miss Hardin?'

Sherry Hardin looked at Frank Angel. She was ready to dig in her heels, to stand alone there against Hugess and all his guns and fight for the three men. He shook his head.

'Go on, Sherry,' he said. 'There's nothing you can do here.'

'But, Frank—' she began.

'Go!' he snapped. Sherry Hardin recoiled from the anger in his eyes, and for a visible moment struggled with tears. Then her head came up again, and without a word she started down the centre of Front Streeet towards the Hotel. Burt Hugess strode alongside her, his gun back in its holster, a challenging scowl on his dark face.

Larry Hugess spoke to Finstatt without even turning his head.

'Take them,' he said. 'Somewhere nobody can hear. Then kill them.'

Without a glance at the three captives, he started off at a leisurely pace down Front Street. Larry Hugess was back in control and it showed in every line of his body.

He had decided exactly what he was going to do and now he did it. He left Sherry Hardin at the Hotel, and told Landy to stay close so that the woman got no wild ideas about going back up the street to see what was happening to

Angel. He had to admit surprise: she was much more woman than he recalled, and his admiration for her had increased tenfold during this short reacquaintance. At one time during the day, watching the proud lithe movements of her body, he had felt the throb of lust for her, imagined her in the moist warmth of a soft bed. Now he had decided that he wanted her, that he would lay siege to her. With a woman like this at his side, there was nothing he could not achieve in politics, in the Capital, anywhere. She would be the toast of Washington. He would dress her in the finest silks, the costliest jewels, the most sumptuous settings. He would put a fine house at her disposal, servants, carriages, all a woman could want. He was still a young enough man to sire children, still handsome enough to win a woman on whom he had set his mind. Typically, it never entered Larry Hugess' mind that Sherry Hardin might not concur with his decisions. And so he had dreamed, in the morning before he had drawn Angel's teeth with his bloodless ruse. Now all that was left was to show this cowed and empty town that Larry Hugess was its king, its emperor, its law, its reason for existence.

He had one of the riders bring up a horse for Burt, and mounted his own fine stallion. Together, they paraded up and down the street for a time, he did not check how long, curvetting on the horses, letting people see them unafraid and unstoppable in the street. When they had had enough of that, Larry Hugess reined in his horse outside the Palace and stalked in. A nervous, stammering Johnny Gardner came up from below the bar, watching their eyes warily.

'Your best champagne, Johnny,' Hugess boomed. 'You've got champagne, haven't you?'

'Yessir,' Gardner said, anxious to please. 'Yes I do, Mister Hugess, sir. Real French champagne. Imported from France.'

'And cold, Johnny,' Hugess said, not emphasising anything but striking fear into the saloonkeeper's heart by the very gentleness of his speech. 'Make sure it's cold.'

'Oh, yes, sir, Mister Hugess, sir,' Gardner said, sweating. 'Oh, yes, sir.'

'You see,' Hugess said, almost dreamily, 'it's kind of a special day. My little brother Burt is coming home today, aren't you, Burt?'

Burt Hugess beamed. 'That's right, Larry,' he said. 'Comin' home.'

He wasn't prepared for the way his brother's face changed, the way the contempt twisted Larry's mouth, the way the eyes looked at him as if he was some filth his brother had found on his dinner plate.

'You don't even know what it cost, do you?' Larry Hugess asked softly.

His riders watched him warily, ready to get out of the way of whatever might happen. They had seen Larry Hugess' soft-spoken rages before: and they preferred hydrophobia skunks on a rampage.

'Listen, Larry,' Burt Hugess said, placatingly. 'I never meant no harm!—'

The flat crack as Larry Hugess hit his brother contemptuously with the back of his hand sounded stunningly loud in the silence. Burt cried out, reeling slightly: bright blood trickled from a split lip.

It had not been a hard blow, only a stinging one, but the contempt in it weighed heavier than if he had been struck by lightning.

'Johnny,' Larry Hugess said, his voice still as soft as swansdown. 'Pour the champagne. Gently, now.' He nodded with satisfaction as Gardner filled the stemmed glasses, watching the way the wine frothed and subsided with visible pleasure.

'Aw, listen, Larry,' Burt Hugess said. 'Listen.'

'Drink your champagne, Burt,' Larry Hugess said. 'And shut your face.'

Four of them.

It could have been worse, Angel thought. Hugess could have sent all seven of his riders down to administer the coup de grace. Then there would have been no chance at all. As it was, he knew that if the guards now prodding them down towards the scarred clay banks of Cat Creek up behind the graveyard knew his thoughts, they would have laughed aloud. Yet Angel, for all his slumped shoulders and air of defeat, was working out just exactly how to take them.

'Down there?' one of the guards said.

'Yeah,' Finstatt told him. 'Then we can just cave some of this cutbank over them.' He might have been discussing where to plant cabbage.

They were approaching the high banks of the creek, which were sharply edged, and fell away almost perpendicularly to the stony dry bed of the stream below – about seven feet, Angel reckoned.

The creek bed was littered with boulders and stones, some of them four or five feet high, rolled downhill slowly with the years of flash flooding, breaking up the dry ground alongside the creek, scouring it with gullies where the roots of sagebrush and greasewood protruded like the buried legs of strange prehistoric birds. He checked the position of the four guards from beneath veiled lids. Two close together nearer him. The others to the left and right of Sheridan and Howie Cade. Too far away to jump.

'Get on down there!' Ken Finstatt snapped.

'Go to hell,' Angel said, pleasantly.

'I said get on down!' Finstatt snarled. 'Unless you want it in the belly now.'

'Just as soon,' Angel said, standing in an almost relaxed slouch that made Howie Cade gape at him as if he had turned into a giraffe.

'All right,' Finstatt said. He came forward and prodded the barrel of his carbine into Angel's belly and that was all Angel had been waiting for.

'Down!' he yelled, hoping to God Sheridan and Cade

would hit the dirt as fast as they could. In the same moment, he grasped the barrel of the carbine, leading it away from his body as Finstatt pulled the trigger. The heat of the muzzle blast burned across Angel's ribs but Finstatt was coming at him now as Angel's hand moved upwards, the heel of his palm forward and his whole forearm braced for the impact.

He hit Finstatt under the jaw, snapping the man's head back and stopping him dead in his tracks, brain jarred into insensibility by the brutal shock of the blow. In the same movement, Angel hit Finstatt just below the heart with his right hand, all his strength and poised weight behind the blow. Finstatt went down as if he had been poleaxed, which, to all intents and purposes he had been, and even as the Flying H man folded to the ground Angel had lifted the carbine out of the nerveless hands and was swinging it in a killing arc that ended alongside the head of the guard in the red shirt who had been closest to Ken Finstatt.

The rifle stock split with a loud crack that blended with the softer, mushier sound of Red Shirt's skull bursting, a sound almost the same as the one made when someone drops an overripe pumpkin two stories down on to a concrete slab. Red Shirt catapulted over the edge of the creek bed without a sound, his head an awful, bloody tatter of splintered bone and oozing brain.

The third guard, a stocky Texan, had time only to turn and face Angel before Angel was on him like a tiger. The Texan had his gun up and was ready to fire but the sight of Angel coming at him as no man he had ever seen coming at him unnerved the Texan and he hesitated that fraction of a second it took Angel to go up off the ground with his feet high, legs cocked like coiled-steel springs that unleashed as fast as the fangs of a striking snake. Both Angel's bootheels smashed into the stocky Texan's face like striking thunderbolts, pulping the astonished visage into a rictus of pain that froze as the man's neck snapped like a dried grass stalk.

Angel hit the ground on his haunches, rolling to one side and kicking at the dusty clay to scare up a cloud of dust that confused the aim of the fourth guard just enough. His first shot whacked up a gout of earth three feet high not six inches from Angel's elbow as the unarmed man came suddenly up off the ground. The Flying H man saw the knife and tried desperately to line up for a second shot but he was a second too late.

Long ago, soon after he'd finished his training with the Department of Justice, Frank Angel had gone to see the Armourer, Charlie Brady. A dour, generally unsmiling man, but there wasn't anyone anywhere, they said, who knew more about weapons. There wasn't anyone anywhere who could come up with a way to conceal a weapon that Charlie Brady hadn't already thought of and, more than likely, discarded as impractical. No weapon Charlie Brady couldn't strip and reassemble in the time it took lesser men to identify the maker. He was the Armourer for the Department and he'd listened without comment to Angel's requests.

Then he had nodded. Not new, he'd said. But adequate. If Angel wanted weapons that would give him a fighting chance for survival in a situation where he had already been disarmed, weapons which would have been overlooked in a reasonably careful search, it would have to be knives. Only fools missed the bulk of a gun in searching a man, and Angel could not rely on Providence pitting him against fools all the time.

'See what we can do,' the Armourer had told him.

He'd come up with a couple of ideas that had suited Angel down to the ground. One of them was the twin, flat-bladed, Solingen steel throwing-knives that nestled snugly in their special sheaths set between the inner and outer leather of Angel's otherwise-unremarkable mule-ear boots. Both were honed to split-hair sharpness and it was one of them that now came up in a tight and remorseless arc, gutting the guard like a trout. He gave a scream like a pig in a slaughterhouse and went over backwards, legs kicking high in agony that ended almost at once. Angel stood, his hands on his knees, bent forward, breath coming harsh and hard, the blood of the men he had killed splattered all over him.

'Jesus, Angel!' Howie Cade said.

He and Sheridan were on their feet now, and they looked around them wide-eyed. The whole thing could not have taken more than two or three minutes, minutes that in the watching had seemed like an eternity. It was like a dream, possible while you were in it, impossible when you woke to think about it carefully. Yet there scattered around them were the dead men and there in front of them was Angel with blood on his hands.

A soft breeze soughed through the greasewood, and despite himself Howie Cade shivered. He watched Angel straighten up, pull in a huge breath, as if preparing himself for some ordeal.

'All right,' Angel said. 'We'd better get moving.'

'What about him?' Sheridan asked, pointing with his chin at the form of Ken Finstatt, huddled in the dusty dirt at the edge of the creek.

'He won't bother us for a while,' Angel said. 'If ever.'

He had cleaned the knife with which he had killed the guard and now slid it back into the scabbard at the side of his boot. He picked up one of the carbines. Howie and Sheridan picked up one each.

'Come on,' Angel said, leading the way across the flat ground, quartering in the direction of the plank bridge at the end of Texas Street, and the rear of the corral behind the general store.

'Where the hell we going?' wheezed Howie Cade.

'Are you kidding?' Angel snapped. 'Where the hell do you think?'

He moved on at a wolflike lope across the empty ground, his eyes on the bayed wagons in the empty corral ahead.

FIFTEEN

'TIME to go,' Larry Hugess told his men.

He permitted himself a smile at the expression of relief that flooded Johnny Gardner's face and which the saloon-keeper quickly stifled in fear. Gardner's reaction was his testing of the town's temperature: they would always be relieved to hear that he was going, never dare to challenge his desire to stay. Madison was his town again. The knowledge gave him a strong, warm feeling in his belly. The whole thing was over. These sheep wouldn't give him any trouble.

He led the way out into the afternoon sunshine and his brother stepped up into the saddle of the horse that had been brought for him. Larry Hugess grabbed the pommel of his ornate saddle and swung aboard the grey. His six riders followed suit.

'I don't see Ken Finstatt no place,' Burt Hugess offered.

'Probably waiting for us up by the warehouse,' his brother replied. He kneed the horse into movement and led the cavalcade across the T-junction of Front and Texas, the Oriental on their right, their shadows long and black on the hoof-pocked street.

Howie Cade stepped into the street: he had a carbine canted across his hip and the barrel of it was pointed straight at Larry Hugess.

'Leavin' so soon?' Howie asked.

The eight men had reined in their horses in astonishment when he appeared. Larry Hugess stared at the deputy as if he truly were a ghost. Before he could speak, a dry cough from behind the group made him swivel his head around. There, in the middle of the street behind them was Dan Sheridan. He had a sixgun in his left hand. It was cocked and pointed at the Flying H men.

'What the hell?' hissed Burt Hugess.

'I'll count five,' Howie Cade was saying. 'By that time I want all your guns and belts in the dirt. One.'

Larry Hugess' mind was as busy as a rat in a maze. He had already considered and rejected half a dozen ploys, asked himself and answered as many questions when Howie counted out the second number.

'All right,' he said.

'Three,' Howie said. 'Let it be nice and easy now.'

'All right,' Larry Hugess said. Then he rolled out of the saddle, his hand yanking out the gun in the holster at his side. The grey, suddenly tortured by the wrenching pull on the *chileno* bit, screamed shrilly and reared up, spooking the other horses into a milling bunch that was galvanised into a flat gallop by the simultaneous explosions of Larry Hugess' and Howie Cade's guns. Howie's shot whacked the rider who'd been immediately behind Larry Hugess out of the saddle in a windmilling pile. At the same time, Larry Hugess' shot hit Cade in the belly, hurling him in a bundle against the solid upright of the hitching rail outside the Oriental.

Burt Hugess and three of the Flying H riders were already moving hard up the street towards the safety of the Hugess warehouse as behind them Dan Sheridan turned loose with the handgun. His four rapidly fired shots sounded flat and undangerous in the open sunlight but one of them tore Stu Fennick out of his saddle, dead before he even hit the ground, and another bored an ugly hole in the leg of Jim Landy before bursting through the leather fenders of his saddle and gut-shooting the roan mare he was riding, knocking the animal into a slewed heap in the street. It lay kicking and whinnying as Landy rolled off the horse and thumbed a shot at Sheridan who was out in the middle of the T-junction and running forward, a movement that probably saved the Marshal's life. Landy's hasty shot tipped the right hand side of the frontal bulge of Sheridan's forehead, cutting a searing burn in his skin and knocking the lawman off his feet, momentarily stunned. In that same moment, Larry Hugess tried for him from the porch of the Hotel, and his aimed slug whined viciously through the space that moments ago Sheridan had been filling.

On one knee, Sheridan pawed away a trickle of blood from his right eye and thumbed back the hammer. His placed shot hit Landy just as the Flying H man was getting clear of the thrashing roan, driving Landy down flat into the unheeding dust. As Sheridan whirled towards where Larry Hugess lay prone alongside the boardwalk around the front of the Hotel, he was knocked off his feet as the whole world went up in the air and came down again.

Frank Angel had planned hastily but effectively. With Sheridan at the back, Howie in the centre, the only direction in which the Flying H boys could break would be towards the depot, and he had anticipated that by running flat out across the open ground behind the saloon and the houses on the eastern edge of Front. Where the pathway down from the church led to Front Street he skidded to a stop. It wasn't more than ten yards from where old Nate Ridlow had been bushwhacked, and Angel's lips curled into a grim smile at the savage irony of what he was going to do. He fired the short fuse on the three sticks of dynamite just as Burt Hugess and the three Flying H riders burst into their desperate gallop towards the safety of the Hugess warehouse. In one smooth sweet movement, Angel lobbed the dynamite he'd taken from Ridlow's wagons beneath the feet of the oncoming riders and went forward on his belly, the carbine cocked, placing his shot squarely through the forehead of Burt Hugess' horse. In that same moment Ed Barth and Bill Wessell yanked their horses back on their haunches, stabbing hands towards the guns at their side and even getting them out in the long, empty moment when it seemed to Angel that the world was holding its breath awaiting the explosion.

The dynamite went off with a solid, heavy, flat bang and a fountain of dirt and dust erupted forty feet into the air in the centre of Front Street. The air was full now of whickering pieces of gravel and softer, wetter things which splattered against the walls of the houses and the Hotel. Every window on the street for twenty-five yards in either direction bulged outwards and then smashed inwards in flying smithereens a thousandth of a second later, filling the air with the jangling clatter of falling glass. Angel could see a man floundering about on hands and knees in the dirt, blood streaking his face and hands. The dust hung like a pall, drifting slowly eastwards across the street, shadowing the sun. As it cleared, Angel could see Burt Hugess off to one side, lying flat on his back not far from the dead body of his horse, which had dropped like a stone on the spot where Angel had shot it. Bill Wessell, blinded by the explosion, was groping around for something familiar to touch not two yards from the flayed corpse of his horse which lay across the tattered remnants of Ed Barth's body. Of the third man, Jack Coltrane, there was no sign at all.

As Angel came running across the street, Bill Wessell pawed enough dirt from his eyes to see the moving figure, and cursing mindlessly, tried to scrabble towards the sixgun he had dropped in the dirt. He had almost closed his fingers around the butt when Frank Angel was on him like a tiger, and the savage sideswipe of the carbine barrel stretched Wessell flat in the dirt, his right leg kicking in reflex, a bright new trace of blood across his broken forehead.

Angel moved fast to where Burt Hugess lay in the dusty street, his hand quickly checking the soft point below the jaw hinge for the reassuring throb of blood in the carotid artery. Nodding, he looked around with narrowed eyes for Burt's brother, but of Larry Hugess he could see no sign.

The street looked like a battlefield.

There were two dead men slumped in inhumanly twisted shapes between where Angel crouched alongside the unconscious form of Burt Hugess and the Palace Saloon. Three dead horses. He shook his head: in those few terrible minutes, the proud strength of the Flying H had been broken like a butterfly by an iron wagonwheel. Where the hell was Larry Hugess?

He saw Sheridan coming up the street on lagging feet, noted the trickle of blood at the Marshal's temple. Sheridan looked exhausted. Angel gave him a wave: okay, it said. The Marshal acknowledged it and instead of coming the rest of the way, veered across towards the steps in front of the entrance to the Oriental, where Howie Cade was now sitting up, holding his belly with hands slick with blood.

The last traces of the dust sifted away and the sun was strong again. When Angel looked up, Larry Hugess was there on the porch of the Hotel and Sherry Hardin was tight close against him, her right arm jerked up high behind her back, her face twisted in a mixture of pain, fear, and chagrin. Larry Hugess had a sixgun barrel jammed into the soft pad of flesh below the girl's chin and the gun was fully cocked.

'Angel!' Larry Hugess hissed.

Frank Angel rose, very slowly, very warily. He kept his hands away from the gun at his side. The carbine he had laid on the ground caught a shaft of sunlight and winked at him mockingly.

'Get away from my brother!' Larry Hugess shouted. 'Get back away!'

Angel nodded. Hands up away from his body, he walked backwards six or seven paces, then stopped. He saw Dan Sheridan start to move towards him from outside the Oriental, and he made a signal with his left hand: stay. Sheridan stood stock still, like a kid playing statues. His eyes moved from Hugess to Angel, back again, weighing the danger, the odds, ready for action.

'He's not dead, Hugess,' Angel said, his voice level and matter-of-fact.

'Not dead?' Larry Hugess' face was a study of disbelief.

'Not dead,' Angel said. 'He's out cold.'

'Uh,' Larry Hugess said, digesting what this meant. Angel smiled coldly.

'That's right, Hugess,' he said. 'He'll stand trial. There's no way you can stop it now. You've lost. Put down the gun and turn Miss Hardin loose.'

'Ha!' Hugess said, jerking Sherry back closer against him. 'You'd like that, wouldn't you?'

'You're through, Hugess,' Angel informed him coldly. 'It's only a matter of whether you want to live long enough to be tried and hung, or whether you want to die right here now.'

'Yes,' Hugess said. 'There's just one thing.' He jerked his chin at his prisoner. 'The girl.'

'What about her?' Angel said tonelessly.

'We do a deal,' Hugess said. 'You let me ride out of here, take Burt. When I'm clear of town, I turn the girl loose.'

'And if I say no?' Angel said, noting the flicker of movement behind Hugess but not showing that he had done so by even so much as the lift of an eyebrow.

'Then I kill her here in front of you,' snarled Hugess. 'I mean it, Angel.'

'Your fight's with me, Hugess,' Angel challenged him. 'Not with the girl. Turn her loose. You've got a cocked gun in your hand. Step away from her – or are you too gutless to take me on even when you've got the drop?'

Anger flared in Larry Hugess' eyes, and for a moment Angel thought he'd do it, but then Hugess shook his head.

'Oh, no,' he said. 'Burt? Burt!'

Burt Hugess was shaking his head from side to side. He began to sit up, his face bewildered like the face of a child who awakens in a different bed from the one he went to sleep in. He heard his brother's voice and turned out of habit towards it.

'Get on your feet!' Larry Hugess snapped at him. 'Go and get two horses! Move, damn your eyes!'

Burt Hugess had gotten to his feet, and his eyes were wide with the horror of a sleeper wakened from a nightmare to find it real. His eyes flicked from one dead body to another, and then to Angel.

'You?' he said, eventually. 'You!'

'Goddamn you, Burt—' Larry Hugess said, but that was as far as he got with whatever he was going to say because at that moment the flicker of movement which Angel had detected in the doorway of the Hotel turned into the reality of the little Chinaman, Chen. Chen had a nine-inch butcher knife in his right hand and he slid it with deft certainty and macabre precision between Larry Hugess' ribs just below the right shoulder blade. Larry Hugess' eyes bulged out like the eyes of a throttled horse, and he went up on his toes, abandoning his grip on Sherry Hardin, who jerked to one side and away. Larry Hugess went down the two steps from the porch into the street on the very tips of his toes, his mouth working and his eyes looking at something that might have been a million miles distant. He tried to lift the gun and point it at Frank Angel while Angel and Burt Hugess stood and watched his marionette approach. Then the spell broke.

A gout of black blood boiled from the rancher's mouth and he pitched forward into the dust. In the same instant, Burt Hugess snatched at the gun in his holster, his burning eyes fixed on the man he desired to destroy with a hatred that was all-consuming: Frank Angel. He was lifting the pistol out of the holster before Angel began to move and a wicked grin of vengeful triumph was already forming on Burt's mouth. Then somehow, astonishingly, inexplicably, he was staring into the barrel of Angel's sixgun before he had eared back the hammer of his own. He stood there with the gun in his hand and knew he was a dead man. He waited for the blasting shock of the bullet but it did not come.

'Go ahead, you mother!' he screeched. 'Do it!'

He tried desperately to will himself to ear back the

mer of the gun in his hand: every nerve in his body screamed with the need to kill the man in front of him. But there was no way he could do it. He stood there in the street, paralysed by his own cowardice, and offered no resistance at all when Angel stepped forward and took the gun out of his hand.

For perhaps two long minutes, they stood there like a tableau: the girl on the porch of the Hotel, leaning slightly forward; the Chinese cook stock still in almost the exact position he had been in when he thrust the knife into Larry Hugess' back; Larry Hugess curiously shrunken in the clotted pool of his own blood on the street; and Burt Hugess and Angel posed like figures in some strange ritual dance.

'It's over,' Angel said. And it was.

SIXTEEN

ENGINE No. 850, *Huntington Carver,* was named for a railroad tycoon. She'd been built ten years earlier in the Philadelphia factory of Matthias Baldwin, a ten-wheeler with a huge, inverted funnel of a smokestack. She was what the railroaders called a 4-6-0, meaning she had four wheels on the lead truck, six drivers, and no wheels beneath the cab. She was pulling a tender and three passenger coaches, and she stood now panting like some sleeping monster alongside the depot in Madison.

Angel went down to say goodbye to Sheridan. Sherry Hardin came, too. She'd left Howie Cade in the care of Mrs. Mahoney, and that fussy old body was giving Howie more tender loving care than he could use. He was going to be all right. The bullet that had torn into his stomach had hit no vital organ, broken no pelvic or spinal bone.

'Clean as a whistle,' Sheridan had complimented him. 'You're a fool for luck.'

'*This* is *luck*?' Howie Cade had said. His face was wan beneath the tan but the smile was about as good as anyone had any right to expect. He had something to aim for now. Sheridan had told him that when he'd delivered Burt Hugess to the Capital, he'd be moving on.

'Where you heading?' Angel had asked.

'I don't know, yet,' Sheridan had replied. 'Seems to me town-tamin's not all it's cracked up to be.'

'Hard way to make a dollar,' Angel had agreed.

'Man like me, though,' Sheridan had mused. 'There isn't much he can do. I done some buffalo hunting. That was all right for a while, but comes a time you can't stand the stink any more, or the slaughter. I'll just drift a while. Maybe I'll find me a place they need a lawman, nice quiet little place with lots of pretty gals.'

'Place like that,' Angel had grinned. 'What do they want with a lawman?'

Now they shook hands gravely and said goodbye without emotion. Burt Hugess was already aboard: safely locked in the caboose and handcuffed to a steel upright. He wasn't about to try anything, anyway. Since the bloody affray in Madison the preceding day, he had been morose and withdrawn, eyes hooded as though he were watching again and again a mental picture of his brother coming down the steps of the Hotel like some weird puppet, all up on his toes as though trying to soften the awful, biting inner rigidity of the scalpel-sharp butcher knife and then collapsing, legs kicking helplessly, in the ankle-deep dust of Front Street.

'Luck,' Angel said to the Marshal.

'And to you,' Sheridan replied. 'You heading out today?'

'I reckon so,' Angel said. 'That fellow I'm chasing's got one hell of a headstart now.'

He noticed Sherry Hardin's head come round sharply as he said this, but he didn't say anything. Sheridan saw it too, and he remained silent.

'Sherry,' he said. 'See you in a few days.'

'Dan,' she acknowledged.

She stood there with Frank Angel, her shoulder just touching his, as the guard gave his shout, the engineer yelled his acknowledgement, and the beautiful ten-wheeler started to move, wheels spinning *shun-shunshun-shun-shun* and then taking their hold on the silver track that stretched to the northeast. The smoke billowed up from the smokestack, laying back over the tops of the carriages as the train picked up speed. Sheridan didn't look back or wave.

When the train was a smudge on the flat land, they walked back down Front Street together. People were out hammering planks over their broken windows: Mahoney's hadn't had anything like that quantity of glass in stock and it would be some weeks before windows could be shipped in from

Winslow. Johnny Gardner was doing land-office business at the Palace: most of the people in town were coming in to hear his account of what he'd heard, what he'd seen, what had happened, and comparing it with their own.

'You meant that,' Sherry Hardin asked. 'About leaving today?'

'I have to,' he said. They stopped in the middle of the street and looked at each other. A woman walking along the sidewalk frowned as if in disapproval. 'You know that.'

'I know it,' she said. 'I always knew it would be like that.'

'You could make it easier for me,' he said.

'That's right,' Sherry replied. 'But I don't think I will.'

'It's my job,' he said to her. 'It's what I do.'

'I'll put you up some food,' she said. 'While you go say goodbye to Howie.'

She turned away quickly and went into the Hotel, but he caught the gleam of the tears in her eyes. He told himself he was being dumb. It wouldn't matter if he stayed one more night. No one would ever know. Not true, he thought: I'd know. And anyway, all I'd have to do would be to do it over tomorrow, or the day after tomorrow, or whenever it was. So it might as well be now.

He still didn't want to go.

He went over to Mrs. Mahoney's and said goodbye to Howie. They shook hands.

'I figured you'd stay around,' Howie said.

'No,' Angel replied.

Howie shook his head.

'Your boss, this attorney-general character you mentioned,' he said. 'He must be some hell of a holy terror, he can booger you into action from that far away.'

Angel thought of the man in the big high-ceilinged room in Washington, of what his reaction would have been had he been able to hear Howie's assessment of him. He grinned.

'You're about right,' he said. 'He's a kind of a hell of a holy terror at that.'

'I never thanked you,' Howie said abruptly.

'Good,' Angel told him. 'Don't start now.'

He went out of there before it got maudlin. You made friends very fast in the kind of circumstances he had walked into in Madison. It was hard just to walk away from them, back to his own lonely life, knowing that in all probability he'd never see them again. He thought he'd quite like to know whether Howie would make out. He figured he probably would.

'I made you beef sandwiches,' Sherry Hardin said, her face just that shade closer to held set than to composed. 'And a canteen of coffee.'

'That's fine,' he said. 'Thanks. Thank Chen for me, too.'

'He didn't make them,' she said.

'Not for that,' he replied. 'I'm not too good at leaving time.'

'Me neither,' Sherry Hardin said. There was a silence.

'This job,' she said. 'How long will it take?'

'I don't know,' he replied. 'Honestly don't know.'

'And when it's over? When you've found this man, Magruder? What then?'

'Then,' he said. 'I'll be coming back.'

'Here?' she said. 'To Madison?'

Her eyes were bright, dancing.

'Here,' he agreed. 'To Madison.'

'Oh, Frank Angel!' she said softly. She stood on tiptoes and kissed him softly on the lips. Then she kissed him properly and didn't let up until they both wanted to. He touched her lower lip with a gentle finger, looked for a long moment at the bright copper glow of her hair. She was a very beautiful lady, and the gift of her love was priceless. How could he do less than fulfil the need that shone from her eyes? He kissed her again, this time for goodbye.

'I'll be back,' he told her. 'You be ready.'